Criminal Intent

A Collection of Writings From Murderous Ink Press

****

Criminal Intent

A Collection of Writings From
Murderous Ink Press

First published by
Murderous-Ink Press
Crowland
LINCOLNSHIRE
England
www.murderousinkpress.co.uk

Paperback Edition ISBN: 9781909498150
eBook Edition ISBN: 9781909498167

Acknowledgements

At this point it is usual to thank those people who have been involved with this. They are many, and all have been invaluable over the years for their input, criticism, advice, yet more criticism, suggestions, and critical observations (aka bloody minded criticism). Sadly not all are still with us to see this come to print.

You know who you are. You will be blessed and/or damned accordingly. This is, after all, all your collective faults.

And to my partner, Den, as always.

Please Note:- All bands, groups and singers, along with all song lyrics quoted in various sections, are purely fictional, and merely indicative of a shared "disgustingly lowbrow taste in music."

Contents

You Make Me Wanna Shoop
(An Editorial of Sorts)

So it's lunchtime on a Saturday. We're 4 months into the CV-19 self isolation. And the landline rings.

I pick it up. At the other end Jack Bateman says something. I say something like, "Yeah, I still have the archive on a hard drive. Somewhere…." From that point on Mr Adrenaline proceeded to slowly beat Captain Common Sense to a bloody pulp with a Louisville slugger.

We're much older, a lot more wiser, yet still full of piss and vinegar. And if you're reading this, oh best beloveds, that is how *Murderous Ink Press* was reborn.

What you have here is akin to the old vinyl record label sampler. A taster of what has already been put out back when Createspace was new, and the expression Sock Puppets had yet to be coined in regard to Amazon reviews.

There's new and original work in here as well. Material from Kelly Lewis, Alice Rothwell, and Dan Meyers all appear for the first, but hopefully not the last time.

We're also in the process of setting up a regular, quarterly, short story anthology series, some themed, some a free-for-all, with anything from Cosies through to Darkside/NOIR between the covers. If it's quality writing then we'll print it.

The MIP motto is simple: You never know what you like until you read it.

So, if you think you may have a piece of fiction we might be interested in – anywhere between 1,000 to 10,000 words – then go across to our website www.murderousinkpress.co.uk read up on the submission guidelines, then go to the Crimeucopia guide page. Those themes are just wide spectrum suggestions, and there is also the 3rd of the annual 4 which is unthemed as well.

While there, you'll also be able to check out the full versions of the three novels already in print. And if you feel so moved, buy something.

And with all of this now done, over the page is where you start to dip into this Murderous Ink – Criminal Intent sampler.

Oliver, Marty and Me
Dan Meyers

"So you think my sister's a whore?"

"Not your sister. Your sister's an angel. I said your mother is a whore."

At the other end of the empty bar, Oliver asks, "Is that conjecture or opinion?"

I swallow the contents of my glass, put it back on the bar top, and look Oliver in the eye. "Neither. Just stating a fact."

Oliver smiles – showing teeth like a long abandoned graveyard. "Well, that makes it indisputable." He slides his empty glass down the bar to me. I line it up with the other two empty glasses and then pour triple shots of vodka into all three.

"Here, see if you can manage to catch the glass this time." I slide his drink along the bar, watching as he barely manages to stop the glass from sliding off the end. He grins like a mule eating garlic. I say, "I've told you, I'm not going behind the bar again to get more glasses just because you want to fuck around." We'd started off with half a dozen highball glasses, then moved on to whiskey tumblers when the highballs became victims of gravity.

I look at my watch. 2:27am. No sirens or flashing lights outside. I'm not too sure if the pool of blood around Oliver's bar stool is getting wider. The tourniquet encircling his left thigh should've been slackened and reapplied over an hour ago. But then, why bother? He's going to lose it anyway. Serves him right for being such a shit getaway driver and wrecking the car. Hell, in thirty years' time that car would've been a classic, had it survived.

I raise my glass and say, "Here's to survival," and take a swig of the clear liquid. Oliver takes some vodka, then says, "Has Marty stopped drinking?"

"Ooops! My bad." I lean over the bar, pick up the third glass, and pour the alcohol as close as I can into Marty's open mouth. He's flat on his back. Hardly surprising considering Oliver put several .38s into him – one I'm sure went through Marty's heart. Some of the vodka goes up his nose, and droplets splash into his still open eyes, but most of it dribbles out the corners of his mouth. Maybe it's time to cut him off if he can't hold his liqueur?

I sit back down on the bar stool, just in time to go through a coughing fit. I wipe my mouth with a napkin. More blood than spittle. What the fuck is it with little old ladies and .22 caliber guns? Oliver's looking at me – his glass paused half way to his lips.

I say, "You shouldn't have killed her. She was probably someone's grandmother."

"Fuck you, asshole. You're lucky she only pulled a .22 out of that bag, and not some old .44 hog leg. That would've gone straight through you. Ripped your spine out and pinned it to the far wall."

It was supposed to have been a simple backwater bank job. Marty had talked us into it one evening two months ago, here in the bar.

*****

"I was passing through there 6 years back, driving on down to the Keys with Michelle. She's the blonde." He points to the row of three framed photographs – his ex-wives club. Each photograph had been pinned to the wall using a nail gun – a nail through each of their foreheads. "Anyway, we're way out in the boondocks, staying in the local hotel for several days, and I got to thinking…."

That's when we should've known it was all destined to fail – using the words 'Marty' and 'thinking' without putting 'you're not' in between the two was a total oxymoron. But we still let him carry on talking.

"There's a big processing plant about 10, maybe 15 miles away, pays its workers monthly by bank transfers. Sort of like electronic cheques."

He pauses, and Oliver calls it first. "You not thinking of hacking the bank transfers are you, you dumb prick? That's just pure Hollywood. Jesus H. Christ!"

Marty gets bitchy. "If you'll just shut the fuck up for a minute? We're not looking at the transfers, or any account details either. We're looking at cash from the local retailers. The bank is the only place in the town that has a satellite link to the internet. Hell, there's not even any cell phone reception out there. It's all old fashioned overhead cables and landlines. No cell provider's prepared to run a service to out-of-the-way Hicksville, so most of the businesses rely on cash that people draw out from the bank – either over the counter, or via the ATM. That means the town has a fair amount of good old re-circulating non-traceable greenbacks sloshing around in the vault."

Oliver's about to say something snarky, so I cut him off at the pass. "I know you're not going to suggest mugging every person we see coming out of the bank, so what's the deal?"

Oliver turns to me. "Are you seriously listening to this guy, Bobby Gee?"

I make the second fuck up of the night. "Can't hurt to hear the man out, can it. Go on Marty, having set the scene, what's the play?"

"With all the usual big city facilities non-existent, when the pay gets transferred to their accounts on the last Friday of the month, most of the citizens withdraw a big wad of it in cash. So we go in on the last Thursday of the month, when the bank's still full of ready money."

I say, "Any bank job needs research, surveillance, scoping out – so it's going to take some time just to put everything like that together."

Marty smiles, all toothpaste and strawberry mouthwash. "Done all that already. Hang around after I close and I'll walk you all through it."

*****

Of course, what could go wrong did go wrong. The latex zombie masks were a size too small and damn uncomfortable even before the three of us piled out of the car. Marty had the lead with some cheap shit Russian pump action shotgun. In through the doors, two in the ceiling, "Everybody down on the floor now!" Oliver and me we're following behind, waving big black 9mm automatics and sweating like a pair of pedophiles in Santa suits.

Only, after the first skyward shot of double-ought, the second one got jammed up with a crunching noise you could've heard all the way back to the State line.

Some people had already dropped to the floor on the first shot, but others had gone to the sides, or dived under nearby desks. Several tellers were looking on behind bullet proof glass while the manager in a lightweight grey 2-piece was desperately trying to punch in the security door combination so he could get through into the back offices.

Next thing I know, Marty's thrown the shotgun to one side, turned and barged between Oliver and me – shouting, "Out-out-out!"

I'm almost through the door when I feel a poke in my back. I turn round, and see a 60-something mom – hair up high and more make-up than a rodeo clown in a dress – standing behind a desk and pointing a chrome .22 revolver. Oliver turns, not even slowing down, and lets one lose. All that training in Helmand finally paid off. She goes down, and I know she's not going to get up again.

We all pile into the SUV Marty had kitted out with fake plates – Oliver driving, me up front, and Marty in the back – and we manage to get the fuck out of town. Didn't even stop when we dumped the zombie masks as we passed the 'Welcome To…. Home of the pickled pig's foot' city limit sign – or some shit like that.

Then it was a long, hard, 12 hour straight drive to get back home. All the way up, Oliver and Marty kept needling each other like a couple of teenagers. I try to sleep, then drive, then try to sleep again – forever feeling a tacky wetness on my back, and a stabbing pain every time I breathe in deep.

Finally, around 1 a.m. this morning, we see the sign *Heggety's Country Bar* up ahead. But the two of them are still verbally tearing chunks out of each other – so much so that Oliver almost misses the turn into the parking lot. He yanks the steering wheel sharply to the left, only he doesn't stop to open the gates first, so we grind to a halt with the gates ripped off their posts and wrapped around the front of the car.

By that time I'm stoically philosophical. Whatever else can get fucked up will get royally fucked up, regardless of what we do.

I climb out, only to find Oliver and Marty are still facing each other in the middle of the car park, both ranting and raving. Then, from nowhere, Marty pulls out a knife, and next thing I know, it's sticking out of Oliver's thigh. In retaliation, he pulls out a little snub nosed .38 and gives Marty two, up close and personal.

Marty does the decent thing for once and drops like a sack of shit, while Oliver finally realizes he still has the knife stuck in him.

I'm now starting to wonder if any of the neighbors heard the crash, or the gunshots. As Oliver puts the revolver away, he says, "Gimme your belt."

"What?"

"Your pants belt. I need it."

So I pull the length of leather with a brass pin buckle out

from around the waistband of my jeans and pass it to him.

Guy doesn't even say 'Thank you.' He just wraps it around his upper thigh, pulls it tight and locks the buckle so it doesn't come loose.

He looks off into the distance and says, "Now for the hard part." And before I can stop him he's yanked the knife out, and for a moment I think the bleeding gets worse.

We both look down at Marty. I say, "Best get him inside."

So we get his keys out of his pocket and drag him into the bar, turn on a couple of lights and drop him behind the counter.

When we're done, Oliver says, "Well, Bobby Gee, this really is one mighty bad SNAFU. Still, I guess Marty's in no position to complain if we help ourselves to some liqueur, now is he."

*****

I take another look at my watch. 2:41am. Still no sirens or flashing lights. I look across at Oliver again. The red around his bar stool has spread. I know because I can see my leather belt hanging loose where he's slackened it off. Oliver carefully drains his glass, then puts it on the bar top, upside down.

"Sorry, Kimosabe," He looks down the bar at me, his eyes heavy lidded and half closed. "I think it's time I finally caught up with my sleep. See you wherever, whenever that might be." He folds his arms on the bar top and rests his head on them.

I go into another coughing fit – the worst so far – screaming pain in my chest, hard to breath in, and the back of my hand is coated in dark red. It'd be nice to just go to sleep, but I've still got one more thing to do.

I rip the pocket off my shirt, soak one end in vodka, and with a book of matches from a bowl on the bar, I set alight to the other end. Vodka doesn't burn unless you heat it, and I figure Marty's soaked shirt would've warmed up from his remaining body heat.

I lean over the bar again, watching the burning cloth and seeing the alcohol start to burn blue. Then watch it drop onto the middle of Marty's shirt. When the flames take hold I sit back down on the bar stool again, involuntarily hawking up a chunk of blood and phlegm, and spitting it into the remaining empty glass.

Every account I've read has always stated that people die of smoke and fumes long before the flames reach them.

I pick up the vodka bottle and pour some over the blood clotting in the glass, turning the whole thing pinkish red. I take a sip, and hope for once that Lady Luck is on our side, and that the Fire Department won't get here in time.

Extract from California Twist
John A. Connor

Prologue

Midnight. The drizzling rain falls gently, sparkling and glittering like crystal dust in the glow from the vandalised street lights. Blue and red neon bleeds across the wet parking lot from the tired and shabby strip mall, while the muffled thump of a bar room jukebox occasionally matches time with the sign's flashing. Whenever the door swings open, the sound jumps out like an angry junkyard dog, before the door closes again, and the music returns to its muted hammering. It's Friday night in the Piederbeck district.

Across from the parking lot the sidewalk edges onto the overgrown front yards of a series of neglected houses, and at the back of Number 43 – old Mrs Mallory's place – the loud opera music starts; then stops again several minutes later. Outside, at the junction, a bus turns left then heads rapidly down the street, engine loud in the ensuing silence, disappearing to leave hollow echoes of noise in the distance.

From somewhere nearby, a night bird starts calling, while from inside 43's back kitchen something makes low, animalistic, mewling sounds.

Splinters of broken glass sparkle on the kitchen doormat where visitors with good manners wipe their feet, before settling down at the kitchen table. Cup of coffee and a slice of pie. Half listening to old man Carmody gossiping and setting the world to rights, while Evangeline Mallory carries on baking as if she were preparing to singlehandedly feed the five thousand.

Tonight, though, things are a little different.

For a start, there wouldn't've been any need to break the little pane of glass by the door handle if she didn't keep leaving the fucking key in the lock.

Over in the corner, by the worktop, the stove is cooling. The kitchen table has been pushed hard up against the sink under the back window, with three of the old beechwood dining chairs tucked neatly underneath it. The fourth had been placed in the centre of the cleared space.

With its arms and legs bound tightly to the heavy wooden frame by lengths of strong plastic washing line, the naked body had, two hours previous, been a young man. Back then the questions had been punctuated with a little slapping, though careful so he wouldn't bite his tongue. Otherwise how would he be able to tell where the treasure was?

But he just kept on repeating the same old, "I don't know anything," story, which soon got to be irritating. I mean, like really irritating, because he knew, and he just kept on lying. Which was a bad, bad thing to do. In the end there had been little choice but to go to the car and get the iPod docking station, the tool roll, and some wide gaffer tape.

Walk back into the kitchen, and without even touching him

he'd started to blub – still making with the lying – until his voice had become as irritating as a nest of tiny red ants, biting and chewing on the nerves. It had been a relief to stuff one of his socks into his mouth, tape it shut, then just listen to the silence before slipping the iPod into the dock and picking out a track. Nothing sets the mood better than a piece of Italian opera for this kind of work....

The small tire iron didn't take long to heat up on the gas stove. It's always satisfying to watch the flame lick the metal, see the tip of it change colour. Turn up the music, nice and loud, the best way to appreciate Rossini's Barber of Seville, then over to stand behind him.

La la la la-la!

Arm around his throat, elbow under his chin, then pull the head up and back.

La-la-la la!

Then bring the tip down onto his chest.

Figaro! Figaro! Fiiiiii-garrrrr-ooooooh!

Boy, could he struggle! Never thought he had it in him, took him to be more a sissy boy. Then the smell of burning, and the curious way his skin and nipple blistered up. Why do men have nipples anyway?

Wait for him to calm down, then pause the iPod. Ask the same questions, over and over again, then push the sock back in, tape him up, then go back to the stove.

Rasori e pettini

lancette e forbici,

al mio comando

tutto qui sta.

Of course, after two hours – doesn't time fly when you're having fun? – he'd first pissed himself, then emptied his bowels – which had been a really serious buzz kill.

Yet even after the branding, the broken fingers, the boiling water on his feet, he'd just kept on lying and lying. Until, hell, it had started to sound like the truth, and he really didn't know where the treasure had been hidden.

But The Man had said that this asshole knew, and it was important to get the treasure back. Find the treasure, get it back to The Man. Because if The Man is happy then everyone is happy. And that is a Good Thing.

Of course, if this asshole didn't know where the treasure was, who did? His girlfriend? His boyfriend? His buddies? Nothing he's said makes any sense!

Be quiet and let me think!

Even the old bitch, Mrs. Mallory, was supposed to have been away on vacation with her beloved grandson. Otherwise there would've been no point in choosing her house in the first place.

Finding her in bed had been a real surprise. With her in her eighties, it had been easy to keep pushing on the pillow until she stopped thrashing about. She had some nice meds on her bedside table, though, which sort of makes up for the inconvenience.

Time to finish up and disappear. Cut a side off a cornflake box, fold it, then tape it over the broken pane in the kitchen door. In this neighbourhood it won't look out of place

Collect up the iPod dock, the gaffer tape and tool roll, take them out to the car and drop them in the trunk. Come back to the kitchen with good old Mr. Longshanks, and a large bottle of Pine Fresh bleach. Stand behind him, legs spread a little for support, hand under his chin, bring his head up and hold it firm. Nudge Mr. Longshanks into the auditory canal, then push-twist-retract – *"It's the rubber grip that makes it non-slip! Mr. Longshanks, the only long shafted screwdriver you'll ever need!"*

Wash and wipe down the scene with Pine Fresh – it always pays to be methodical, that way we don't get caught. Before leaving, put all the stove burners on low – get the kitchen nice and warm. With the sunny weather to help as well, it won't be long before he – and old grandma Mallory upstairs in her bed – would be wriggling fit to bust.

At 3:00 a.m. the bar across the road closed and locked its doors. Patrons and staff wandered off down side streets, or got into cars, vacating the parking lot as they made their way home. One more nondescript car, moving into the flow, rapidly became as invisible as the rest.

1

Late October, and the Sunday evening was cool, clear and dark.

I was in the ground floor living room, the lights turned low, sitting in an old leather club style easy chair. The light from the hearth had died down, and out beyond the patio windows, above the canyon rim and the dark forest line, I could see masses of distant stars. Like most Boy Scouts, I could pick out the better known constellations, but that was as far as my astronomical skills went.

The logs settled noisily in the hearth, and the rekindled firelight made new-born shadows dance around the open plan room. Three fingers of something amber and smooth in a whiskey tumbler rested comfortably in my hand. As Lonnie Tewkes' slow trumpet flowed like warm, rich chocolate from the stereo, I told myself that it was time to move on.

Plenty more fish in the sea…

Plenty more pebbles on the beach…

Plenty more frogs in the pond…

Ah, who was I kidding?

Being dumped sucked.

Big time.

*****

Monday morning, and although I'd been back in the US for some time, I'd never grown out of the British habit of driving with a stick shift. Oncoming traffic had cured me of driving on the left side of the road, and although I will always miss roundabouts, I really appreciated the advantages of turning right at a red light.

Still, the drive into the city from Concrete that Monday seemed longer than usual. Not that I time myself, you understand, but there were unconscious markers between the CD in the stereo – this time it was Vicky LaPerso, the 1956 Ventura sessions – and how far I'd been able to travel down the just-getting-choked-up traffic queues heading into the city itself.

"Gonna buy me some deadly poison, baby!

Gonna mix it up,

With some strong gin!

Gonna buy meeeeep– !"

Taking my finger off the eject button, I pulled the CD from the slot and tossed it onto the back seat. The last thing I needed right then was a self-pitying, "Oh, woe is me," attitude. I blindly rummaged in the scatter on the passenger side, and moments later another CD was sucked into the player's waiting maw. Cranking down the windows and cranking up the volume, I let the Jinxtones take wing and scare a couple of teenagers in their open top Jeep, stuck in the next lane to mine.

"How you call all your lover-boys? White TRASH!"

Yeah, tell it like it is, Danny. Tell it like it is.

Out of boredom, I watched as several drivers started talking to themselves. Around here that usually meant they were either off their medication, or on hands-free and their cell phones had locked onto a stable signal. Given the scant coverage, and with no intention of installing masts, most of us Concretes don't bother with cell phones much. It's always been one of the town's saner attractions.

With a population approaching two and a half thousand, the small town of Concrete, Northern California, lies strung out, in, and around a long canyon. Access was by a bunch of back roads which, in turn, eventually connected to Highway 299. From there it was only a hop, skip and a fender bender away from the Interstate – the good old I-5.

The first settlement had originally been named after the

bird, the Corncrake, way back in the 1850s. In those crazy gold rush days, when all around were striking it rich, the best the town could come up with was pyrites and dust. So it diversified into whiskey and brothels. Times were good and the money kept rolling in.

However, when the gold ceased, so did the town. Dead and dormant – a fitting tribute to the equally dying Wild West – it became just another Northern Californian ghost town. That was until 1910, when Dr. Theodophilous P. Jacksonhammer founded his Resort of Health & Inner Beauty. The good Doctor, formally a philandering snake-oil specialist from Alabama, discovered that by the judicious use of assorted herbs and compounds – which, years later, topped various Narcotic & Controlled Substance lists – he could easily part his patrons from their parents' money. This he used for the advancement of his own research into luxury living.

Like the whores and hoteliers of the previous age, when the scam finally came to an end, he took the money and hightailed it back over the state line – leaving the old ghost town with a new ghost spa. In those days the ghosts never had it so good.

The Depression, the Second World War, the Edsel and the Hoola Hoop, all dropped in and out of fashion during the next lull in the town's time line. It wasn't until the Summer of Love regenerated old smoker myths of a forgotten Nirvana, that a slow but regular trickle of hippies and other free thinkers start migrating from the east – giving a whole new meaning to the term, Way Out West. Especially when it was discovered that several generations of Narc-less and Fed-less interference had let the good doctor's gardens of *Cannabis sativa* and *Erythroxylum coca novogranatense truxillense* grow wild.

Once the rumours had been confirmed, people were eager to repopulate the area.

After the Summer of Love, there came the Winter of Discontent. Biker gangs had found easy pickings from the land and the nearby towns, until their activities attracted the attention of the County Sheriff, as well as the city police. In true Wild West tradition, they arrested any and everything that moved, in as short a time as possible, leaving the ghost town to itself once more – albeit now with a mescaline-aided Make Love, Not War makeover.

Today, Civilisation is slowly rediscovering the legal joys of living out in Concrete. Businesses have started to come out here, and the mail service delivers to the community on a daily basis, so somebody must know we're here to stay – even though most of us have to go to the city in order to earn a living.

After a slow hour of stop-go-stop-go car shuffling, I turned onto Chancery, then into the cool of the underground car park beneath the Kincade Building. It's a classy address, I'll give you that, and my old Ford PoS always looked out of place among the BMWs, Jags and Toyotas. But it's where I work. Well, to be more exact, it's where I come when I don't have work.

I parked in my regular Visitors Only bay, eased my six foot one frame out of the car, and stretched a little to un-kink some of the muscles in my shoulders. Safe in the knowledge that no one, in their right mind, had enough sympathy for me to steal the damn vehicle, I took a steady walk over to the building's elevators.

These days, taking the stairs is considered the healthier

option, but I just can't get excited over it. True, not everyone has their own home gym, but after fifteen years of active military service, such things as regular exercise are ingrained into my subconscious. Anyway, after the first eight floors, stairwells become passé – and at my age I've seen more than enough stairwells to last me a lifetime.

Then again, the ride up to the 10th floor had never failed to impress me. The scenery shifts from underground car park to grass and trees as the elevator climbs above ground to street level, then it travels up the outside of the Kincade Building. Some people always faced the wall, in order to avoid vertigo from the height and the view, but I still got a schoolboy kick of excitement every time. The whole block was an innovative award winning design, for its time, constructed completely out of recycled materials. From the reconstituted cement and steel in the walls, to the recycled plastic and glass for the windows. True, when it's kicking over 98 degrees outside, you're thankful for the air conditioning, but at least some of the construction was ecologically sound.

On the way up, the floors and businesses were announced by a calm and emotionless feminine voice, and I wasn't sure if it was designed to tell you where you were or, by omission, who had ceased trading. However, with both the 9th and 10th floors occupied by Orion & Nadler Investigations & Security, I was sure they were going to be around for some time to come. Mind you, I have a vested interest – they throw work my way from time to time.

When the elevator reached the 10th, I stepped out into the open plan reception area and nodded a cheerful "Good Morning!" to Michelle and Darlene, the regular daytime receptionist staff. Michelle smiled and gave a little wave back while still talking into her headset. Darlene silently mouthed something impressively gross before continuing her conversation. "I can really empathise with your grief, Mrs. Gorretski. Believe me, I truly can."

I took a quick time out and looked over the maze of cubes and walkways. It's a sight which reminded me why I never wanted a proper 9-to-5 job.

Muted, bland cubical walls. Neutral cord carpet the right shade of nondescript. Constant overhead lighting, despite all the natural light from the building's three glass sides. Heads bobbed, telephones chirped or berrrrrring'd, keyboards clattered, and photocopiers made those noises only photocopiers do when in captivity. The only thing missing was the rattle of chains and the sound of a drum slowly beating time while an overseer called out, "Stroke!" Still, as I headed towards my office, the call centre operators seemed to be smiling and happy – going about their daily tasks of righting wrongs, ensuring people were protected, and referring callers to others who might be able to help with their questions.

Architecturally, the floor plan closely followed the shape of the Kincade Building itself, which had been designed by several ergonomics experts. The layout was based on a right angle and although I'm not a child of Sesame Street, it always gave me the impression of a big, fat, capital L. From the reception area, you entered around the middle of the down stroke, with two vending machines and coffee break areas at the top. Travelling down the L you came to a water cooler and an office waiting area, off to your right, before the corridor bent 90 degrees to the left.

At the far end of the base, there was a fourth, smaller alcove, on the left, with a single water cooler and just enough space for two adults to hide in, at a push, at, say, an office Christmas party…. Let's just leave it at that.

Walking along the base, I loitered in the alcove by the water cooler, pulled a cup from the dispenser and let water slowly trickle into it. Across the way I could see the old-fashioned dark varnished door, with a frosted glass top panel – incongruous in the modern office environment. The matt gold lettering was tastefully arched, and in classic old style lettering, it read: Mr. Harry Rhimes.

That's me. A little old fashioned, a little retro. It helped keep the kids on their toes, not knowing if I was just a touch eccentric, or completely loony tunes.

Underneath my name was: Private Investigator.

I've always felt it had a classier ring to it, when put like that. More upmarket and respectable than Private Eye. And there's no way I'd ever have Private Dick beneath my name, no matter how fancy the lettering. A touch eccentric, maybe, but certainly not a certifiable screwball. And anyhow, my name's not Richard.

I was contemplating bittersweet memories of mistletoe and gin-tainted minty breath, when a female voice beside me asked, "Is he in yet?"

She was young, late 20s to early 30s, and I guessed around five nine in flat shoes. Her mousy brown hair was cut in a short, tomboy style, which gave her face an elfin look, reinforced by intelligent brown eyes and small nose. She was neatly dressed in a white blouse and a modern no-nonsense two piece, in dark navy wool. Power dressing, but without the coldness to pull it off successfully. Her shoes and shoulder bag matched, but gave the appearance of being an afterthought, rather than by calculated design. She'd carefully applied a minimum of make-up, which highlighted rather than hid her natural complexion, and made for a refreshing change. Attractive, in a girl next door sort of way, if that's what you found attractive.

She appeared impatient and in a hurry, dividing her attention between the closed door, her watch, and glancing down the corridor. Annoyed, she pursed her lips, then bit lightly on the bottom one.

Between sips of water, I asked, "Have you knocked?" I tried, but failed to make eye contact.

A mixture of anger and frustration flashed across her face. "I …!" Then she half turned and took a hesitant step, as if she was about to leave.

I coughed politely. "Perhaps I can help?" I took her by the arm and walked up to the door. Without stopping, I turned the handle and strode in, trailing the young woman behind me.

My office was small and oblong, like a shoebox in comparison to the surrounding floor space. In keeping with the trend, it had been done out in the same bland, oatmeal-tasting colour scheme as the rest of Orion & Nadler. At the far end sat an old oak desk and in front of it was an executive leather chair. Behind it, with its back to the large picture window, was its partner. Thankfully the office faced north, which kept things cool in the summer and, in the winter, helps to steal light off the south facing skyscraper opposite. I got to see the world reflected off its frontage, the windows reminiscent of a large bank of TVs. Sometimes I would spend an hour or two, sitting in contemplation, just looking at the sights reflected back at me.

Half a dozen drab grey filing cabinets along one wall provided a resting place for the coffee maker which, in true office fashion, was always nine-tenths empty and in need of refilling. Humming away to itself, in the corner by the window was a small refrigerator, the sort you find in the not so cheap but still sleazy motel rooms. It usually contained a can of not-so-fresh ground coffee, a plastic tub of sugar and some powdered creamer in a jar for people who felt they needed it. Alongside that I kept a dozen bottles of water, plus several brands of lite beer, for when I needed it.

I picked up the empty coffee carafe and pointed to the chair in front of the desk. "Make yourself at home."

I took some water from the refrigerator, reloaded the machine with the makings, and set it off to do its drip-drip-drip magic as she watched in silence.

Hospitality thusly taken care of, I sat behind my desk, pulled a yellow legal pad towards me and selected a pencil from the desk caddy. I eased back in the chair and said, "Now that civilization has been restored, what can I do for you, Ms.?"

She looked at me incredulously, and sounding slightly bewildered, she asked, "You're Mr. Rhimes?"

"Often imitated, but never bettered." I gave her a reassuring smile. Maybe she didn't appreciate the trapdoor spider approach to client gathering?

Another show of indecisive lip biting, then, "My name is Lindsey Fairfax." She stared down at the edge of the desk. "I want to hire your services. I need you to find someone for me."

In a large script I wrote Missing Person at the top of the legal pad.

"Does he have a name?"

She looked surprised. "How did you…?"

"Most people want me to find something, or someone. You didn't qualify it with brother or sister, father or mother, and you're not wearing a wedding ring so I just assumed it was a friend or fiancé." I gave her a friendly shrug.

She sighed a little. "Well, he's my fiancé – or was going to be, before he disappeared."

"And does he have a name?"

She looked flustered, then shook her head as if to clear it. "I'm sorry, I seem to be going at this all wrong – I probably even sound like a crazy person, but I'm not. I know he wouldn't just leave without…."

I let her trail off and gather her thoughts.

Getting up I asked, "Coffee? How do you take it?"

"Thank you, yes. I prefer it strong and black."

I busied myself filling two mugs, taking my time, and allowing her to compose herself once more. Getting comfortable again, I smiled in an attempt to get her to relax. "Tell me about him."

"His name is Preston Llyle, that's Llyle with three L's. His father is Roger Llyle, the business entrepreneur, though his mother – Margaret – is Roger's second wife. Preston still gets an allowance from his mother, even though he's twenty-five." Conscious of how that sounded, she quickly added, "But he's involved in some businesses himself, so he's not living solely on family handouts."

"Do you have a recent picture of him?"

She looked at her hands as she started to worry at the shoulder bag in her lap – her fingers twisted at the catch. "He's very self-conscious about people taking his picture. I tried to get him on my phone once, but he was so upset I immediately deleted it. The only thing I have is this." Opening her bag, she withdrew a small four by six photograph and placed it on top of the legal pad.

The picture showed half a dozen young men out on a football field somewhere, all dressed in dirty, sweat-stained uniforms. From their frozen positions it was clear they were breaking away from a professionally posed shot, and only half realised someone else had been taking a picture. It was very much a post-game snapshot and, from the scattered background crowd, I assumed it had been taken not long after the final quarter. In the foreground, the players' faces were flushed, their bodies still pumped full of adrenaline. Most had their helmets off, their hair mussed up, damp and clinging from sweat or from having water bottles emptied over them. One of the jocks had two of his fingers taped together; another had been caught in the process of spitting out his mouth guard. All were either smiling, or laughing, eyes bright with success. The downside was it had all the blurriness of a candid shot, taken with an unsteady smartphone camera, making it difficult to distinguish any real detail.

She pointed to the one with the protruding mouth guard. "That's Preston. He said it was taken about three or four years ago."

"Can I keep this?"

"No, it's…" Self-conscious again, her teeth white against her upper lip as she bit at the bottom one, two or three times, then, "I'd rather you made a copy."

"No problem." I picked up the phone and pressed a button. Darlene answered, using her professional voice, "Orion and Nadler, how can I help you?"

"Darlene, could you come by my office; I need something copying."

Without changing her tone she said, "Get screwed," then hung up on me.

Looked like I was going to have to tangle with the photocopier myself.

I eased my shoulders and rubbed the back of my neck a couple of times. Something felt out of sync somewhere, but I wasn't sure what. She was a pretty, organised, and clearly intelligent woman. Yet here she was, emotionally confused over this guy's actions – at odds with her initial image.

"Why do you want to find him, Ms. Fairfax? You're not–?"

"Pregnant?" Anger and resentment flashed across her face. Cheeks flushed, she looked out the window. "Why does everyone think the worst of our relationship? His parents. My parents. You…?" Again her voice trailed off, and I thought she might finally crack and show more of her real self. Holding back her anger was doing her no favours.

Sitting back, I held up my hands defensively. "Hey, I've got to ask awkward questions, no matter how intrusive they seem. It's the way I get to find out things." I took a long breath before continuing. "So I take it you're not pregnant?"

"No." She glared at me like a truculent child.

I let it pass, and moved on with the questions. "And you were engaged?"

She fidgeted, now mildly embarrassed. "Preston said he was going to talk to his family, assure them it wasn't just an impulsive decision on our part, and that we were genuinely committed to it. In a way I can understand the family's concerns. Preston stands to inherit a large part of the Llyle fortune, especially after the death of his half-sister, Jacqueline."

In the back of my mind, something nudged me about the name, Jacqueline Llyle, but I didn't want to break the rapport building between us.

Lindsey continued, "She killed herself just over twelve years ago."

"Much to the delight of the local newspapers who dredge it up on a regular basis." The media always loved an anniversary.

She nodded. "He's the only child from his father's second marriage."

I brought us back on track. "Did Preston actually propose to you? Give you a ring?"

"Not officially, no, but he showed me his grandmother's diamond wedding ring, and said he would get it resized for me once his parents agreed to the engagement." She looked at her hands worrying the snap clip of her bag again.

And there it was. The shell, partially peeled away, revealed the confused child beneath, thrown head-first into the grinder of life. Wearing big girl shoes meant you got big girl problems, whether you liked it or not, and I wondered if she was going to release some of the pressure and start crying. She opened her bag, pulled a fresh tissue from it, delicately blew her nose, and tucked the tissue into the bag. Then the shell was snapped back in place. Maybe later, somewhere more private, I'd get to see the real her again, but for now it was back to business.

"How much does it cost to hire you, Mr. Rhimes?"

I jotted a figure on the legal pad, and turned it around so she could read it.

"That's per day, plus expenses."

She sounded slightly taken aback. "I've got some savings I can transfer…." Another bite of her lower lip. "I can pay you for two days, provided the expenses aren't excessive." She looked back at the pad as if it were a complex math problem.

Giving her more time to think, I reached across the desk, picked up my forgotten mug of coffee, blew on it for effect, then took a large mouthful. It was lukewarm and bitter, just like most of my own failed relationships, and I wasn't prepared to start walking down that road again. It would only take me back to the land of depression, and me, myself and I had made a unanimous decision to move on.

Swallowing hard, physically and mentally, I coughed lightly to regain her attention. "Okay, look, here's what I'll do. I'll find out what I can over the next couple of days. I'll report back to you at the end of each day, and you can cover the expenses once your money's transferred."

In my head I heard my late father's sonorous banker voice calling me a fool. So maybe the next client would be the one destined to bring in the millions. I just wanted to give her a break, is all.

She looked at me to see if I'd meant what I'd said. Then the shell cracked a little again, and the innocent peeked out and smiled – happy in the knowledge that Bad had been vanquished from her life once more. Well, for the next 48 hours, at least.

She dipped into her bag, pulled out a chequebook and a slim silver ballpoint, then wrote out a two day retainer. She tore the cheque free and started to thank me, but I got up, walked around the desk, and handed her a business card from the holder by the phone.

With her chequebook back in her bag, she jotted down a phone number on the legal pad, then wrote 'Lindsey Fairfax' beneath it and ensnared both name and number with a circle.

"That's my home number. I work for Claite Electronics, up on Palmetta, but they don't like employees taking private calls. I've a new Smartphone, only it keeps breaking down and I haven't had time to exchange it yet." Then, with genuine emotion she added, "I really am grateful for this."

I picked up the photograph from the desk. "I'll drop this back to you with the first report, sometime tomorrow evening."

She nodded her thanks and, as I opened the door for her, she paused to look at the photographs and prints on the wall.

On one side, a surreal still life and a couple of abstracts rubbed shoulders with a framed copy of my licence. On the other, a framed clipping from the London Evening Standard, which displayed a picture of one Major H. Rhimes, of the Reds & Royals. Next to that were several photographs of my late Uncle Nathan, on my father's side. One of them showed him beside Jack Orion, shaking hands over the business agreement which had founded Orion & Nadler back in 1958.

The newspaper clipping was from July 1st 1997, with the caption "The Handing Back of Hong Kong." It's one of the few things I'd kept which still tied me to my former life.

She pointed at the clipping. "Is that you?"

I stood to attention, and saluted smartly. "At your service, ma'am!"

She giggled a little, which I appreciated, then I escorted her back to the main reception area, making sure she was on her way before going to the Reception desk.

Thankfully Darlene was away, taking a break somewhere. Michelle smiled warmly at me as I asked if she would make several copies of the photograph. It's not that I don't like modern photocopiers – they just have a pre-programmed aversion to working for me.

Waiting for Michelle to return, I slipped through the fire doors and into the stairwell. The heat from the midday sun hit me as I looked down at the street below. With her image still fresh in my mind, it was easy to pick Lindsey Fairfax out as she stepped off the kerb and crossed the street, heading north – a dark blue blob in a sea of shifting colours.

It's been known, as far back as Jung and Freud at least, that the human mind gains pleasure and peace from patterns. We have a need to make sense out of chaos, and create order out of randomness. Which was why it was easy for me to spot the tail.

I couldn't tell if it was a man or a woman, but no matter how good they were, their lack of variation gave the impression they were somehow tethered to Lindsey. She dodged to the left, so did the tail. To the right, and the tail followed as if on a leash. What clinched it was when Lindsey stopped to get something out of her bag. Oblivious to the flow, other pedestrians were forced to dodge and swerve around her in their efforts to keep going about their business. In such confusion, a second stationary object stood out all the more.

I was surprised to see it was just a solo operator. A good double act would have crossed and re-crossed their paths without hesitation, in order to avoid detection. But with no second to take over, the job of tailing someone was infinitely more difficult. And all the more detectable.

As I saw her move off again, I didn't think she would've considered the possibility that someone was following her. Why should she? She'd struck me as intelligent, resourceful, but naïve in some respects. Had the Llyles sicced an investigator onto her? It was clear someone was carrying out a background check. And now her visit to Orion and Nadler would be logged and filed in a report. Great. Just what I needed.

There was nothing I could do about her tail, or to tip her off. Even if I'd taken one of the elevators and kept track of them on the way down, I would've still ended up losing them at ground level. So I watched as they disappeared further into the madding crowd, then I headed back through the fire doors. I crossed the reception area, and stopped at the front desk to collect the photo and the copies from Michelle. In my absence Darlene had returned. She looked at Michelle, then gave me the skunk eye as I started to walk away. Thus, with my life fulfilled, I headed back to my little office.

2

It didn't take long for me to track down the information I wanted. Surveillance companies often have the ability to deploy a diverse number of investigators. But sometimes a client might prefer to keep things simple, or be forced to use a smaller firm due to cost, or availability.

After an hour of checking business entries and phoning around, I finally got lucky. Tina Parker's smooth voice answered on the third ring. "Parker Detective Agency, how can we help?"

I tried to sound casual and bored, killing time before taking lunch. "Hi Tina, its Harry. Is Dawson there? Nothing important – if he's busy I can call back another time."

"Hi Harry!" Tina changed from professional to warm and friendly. "No, Husband Number Four isn't here right now. He was out early this morning. A client at a legal firm hired him to follow someone for a while. He's been doing it for a couple of weeks now. You want me to pass a message on?"

Still with the casual tone, I said, "No, nothing in particular. Just a social call before I head out to an interview. When you see him, tell him I'll call him next week." I didn't want to seem ill mannered, but I needed to free up the phone. "Oh, I've got another call. You never know, it might be a new client. 'Bye

Tina."

She managed a confused "Er, yeah, 'bye Harry!" just before I cut her off.

To the left of the phone I have a Newton's Cradle, something which had fascinated me since childhood. I reached over, lifted one ball then released it. Every action has a reaction.

To the left of the cradle is a fancy digital clock set in a glass pyramid, which had been a present from an old friend. It showed the time in large black figures on an LCD display. Running off everlasting batteries, it automatically received a time signal from a government funded radio station deep in the Nevada desert which, no doubt, doubled as a telephone exchange for our little green friends from Alpha Centauri. The display told me the time in Beijing was 01:17. Provided I remembered Beijing was 15 hours ahead of California, then it was accurate to the millisecond.

Sure, there was a way of changing the time zone – and the procedure was bound to be simplicity itself – but the manual had been de-stapled and gleefully fed to the shredder after the fourth or fifth abortive attempt.

I shook my head. Maybe, one day.

At 01:21 the phone rang.

Picking it up I said, "Hi Dawson." From the background noise, I could tell he was outside on a street, using a cell phone, and probably trying not to attract attention to himself.

"Hi Harry. Tina just called. Don't have to be a rocket scientist to join up the dots. Tell you what; you show me yours, and I'll show you mine. You first."

I set the Newton's Cradle in motion again – two chrome balls this time – as I pretended to consider his offer. Freud would've had a field day. "Okay. I've got a missing boyfriend and I'm curious as to why you're tailing my client. I saw you from on high. I was up on the tenth floor."

"You must have damn good eyesight."

"Yep. I eat a lot of carrots."

"So do rabbits, but most of them never see what hits 'em."

I smiled. Dawson Parker was a typical easy going West Coast sort of guy, and I knew the banter was helping him kill the boredom of surveillance.

"C'mon, Dawson, ante up – what you got?"

"Two weeks of aching feet. I pick her up in the morning, she goes to work, and I hang around doing coffee and Danish until the evening when she leaves to go home. I keep an eye on her, usually until around midnight, then I'm off the meter until I pick her up again in the morning. For about the first ten evenings she goes out. Does the rounds of several restaurants and bars, asks if anyone's seen some guy, then back home, thankfully before the witching hour. But last Saturday something changed and all she did was stay at home. Guess she figured on getting professional help?"

"Well, she hired me for a couple of days." I paused, waiting for Dawson to crack a funny, but he remained silent so I moved the conversation along. "Don't suppose you could keep me out of your log? Just that it might mess with a particular line of enquiry."

"Well, you know what I'm like for neat and tidy paperwork, Harry. If I start changing it now it'll mean annotating stuff in the margins, or scratching in some kind of footnote. Far easier for me to just leave the entry as 'Visited Kincade Building, floor unknown,' and leave it at that."

"Thanks, Daw. That's one I owe you."

"Ha! Get in line buddy. Talk to ya later."

Gathering the coffee mugs, I went to the restroom and rinsed them off. As I dried my hands, I looked at myself in the mirror. Was I turning into the world's biggest cynic, or did my apprehension about Preston Llyle come from a subconscious dislike of the man?

Maybe Lindsey's emotional shell was there for another reason?

Whatever it was, she was confused and hurt – and desperate enough to hire me.

I waved the mugs dry under the air blower and wondered if the obvious answer was the right one – that she really was a gold-digger just after Preston's money.

I walked back to my office, put the mugs back on their tree, and sat at my desk. With the restrictions imposed by Lindsey's limited funds, I was left with little choice. It was going to have to be quick and dirty if I was to meet the deadline.

Picking up the receiver, I hit one of the speed dials. The phone purrrped several times before the far end picked up.

"Hello Harry." The voice in my ear was smooth, low and female. Elizabeth.

In many respects, to me she remains an enigma. She'd arrived in Concrete one evening on a Yamaha Royal Star, accompanied by David Frederic Earl. He's a white-haired Harley Davidson fanatic who had more than a passing resemblance to Hulk Hogan. In addition to his business skills, a framed certificate proclaimed him to be a fully ordained and licensed reverend of the Holy Moly Rolling Church of the Born Again Brotherhood. They were based out of Modesto, California. Where else? Whether Freddy actually believed in it, or not, was between him and his maker. It meant he could legally perform marriages – Las Vegas style if requested – which was always a profitable sideline to their hospitality business.

The pair had successfully purchased and renovated a derelict three storey hotel. Previously known as Missy Mae's Cat House, they had given it the more respectable name of The Star & Belle.

At first the community didn't know just what to make of the new couple, especially given Concrete's biker gang past. But most of us believed the refurbished hotel would be good for the tourist business in our trickle of a backwater. So Elizabeth and Freddy were readily accepted into the Concrete community.

It was also a strictly business relationship. Freddy managed the hotel, while Elizabeth took on such activities as tracking, survival and woodcraft adventure holidays. She was good at it, too. I suspected she was ex-military, but something more than just your run-of-the-mill G.I. Josephine.

She also knew how to gather information quickly, all of it quality, on a don't kiss, don't tell, cash only basis.

From the receiver, her voice asked, "I take it this isn't a social call, Harry?"

"I'm about to start working a missing persons, and I need

some of your time and expertise." This time of year, with the tourist trade down to nothing, I knew any extra was appreciated. And what the IRS didn't see, the heart didn't grieve over.

"You know you only have to ask, Harry." Soft and low. It was the sort of voice which made telephone sex profitable.

I had seen her clear 100 rounds at her private firing range. Five different weapons, three fixed and one rotating target. Her score was debatable – either 99 or 100 hits – if you believe two rounds went clean through the same hole.

Handguns or rifles, she was equally at ease with either, and The Star & Belle had regularly staged the annual Shoot The 'Nads Off a Gnat at a Thousand Yards tournament for the last five years. Those type of events had little appeal to the rest of us Concretes, but they brought a much welcomed supply of dollars all the same.

"I need some background on a guy – Preston Llyle. He's the privileged offspring of Roger Llyle."

"That's a little judgemental, but I'll assume Roger is the patriarchal head Llyle International. Very upmarket, Harry. Sounds like you're widening your circle at last. How detailed do you want the report?"

"I'm on a shoestring budget and a forty-eight hour deadline. In other words, it's quick and dirty at best, as I need it ASAP."

"I'll see what I can do, but no promises."

"Does that mean I get a discount?"

"Ah, Harry. Despite the world recession, the wages of sin remain the same – as do my rates."

We agreed on a price, then she hung up. That was the easy part.

I spent the rest of the afternoon getting the number for Roger Llyle's personal assistant. He sounded pleasant with an Ivy League accent, so I added a dash of English to help level the playing field.

"Would it be possible to interview Mr. and Mrs. Llyle for a series of freelance articles I'm putting together? The working title is The Great American Good."

He said something polite, then put me on hold. There was a short burst of audio disharmony, which had possibly been music in another life, then his voice came back on the line.

"Would tomorrow morning suit? Mr. Llyle has a free slot between 10:30 and 11:30, and both Mr. and Mrs. Llyle will be happy to see you at that time."

"One moment while I check my planner."

I put him on hold, doodled on the legal pad, then told him 10:30 would be fine by me. He asked for my licence plate so house security could recognise my car, then bid me a cheerful good afternoon.

I drank more coffee, gazed out at the office block across the way, and thought some more about the questions I wanted to ask. My plan of action was simplicity itself. Talk to the parents, find where their son was, and why he'd decided to remove himself from Lindsey Fairfax's life.

In an ideal world, I would find the missing boyfriend, discover it was all a mistake, right the wrong, be invited to the kids' wedding and we'd all live happily ever after.

In an ideal world.

By the time I'd finished staring at Window World, it was heading towards evening and I was ready to go home. The yellow legal pad was now covered in numbers, names and times – along with several doodles of daisies, an oval football, and something which could've been a house. In amongst the scribbles was Lindsey's handwriting. Her figure sevens had the distinctive European bar through the stem, so you couldn't confuse them with her ones.

I took a business card from the desk holder, flipped it over, and wrote her name and number on the back – mimicking her ones and sevens, her precise threes and sharp fives. They brought back memories of my father's notations. He had always insisted my handwriting be legible and distinct, regardless of how quickly I wrote.

Tearing off the top sheet, I jotted out a brief précis of the day's events – more an aide memoir – so I had something to hand over once her 48 hours were up. Later I'd type the pages into the office computer and do my best to make it presentable, though I doubted it would be longer than a page. Two at best. Aside from some dollars for gas, I didn't think I was going to charge her any extra for lunch money.

I spent the next half an hour contemplating Window World again, wondering who worked behind which window, while slowly sipping a Mandel Lite beer from the bottle. I hadn't eaten anything since breakfast, and the cold beer felt warm in my stomach.

Maybe tomorrow would bring the million-dollar client and, naturally, I would be out chasing runaway grooms for disillusioned brides.

The drive back home was easier once I was out of the city

and into the countryside. For me, the best part was seeing the cement and glass give way to trees and open spaces.

I let my right hand diddle with the radio, found several shit-kicker and bluegrass stations, but decided life was too short and the evening too beautiful to go driving myself off of any nearby cliffs. Tuning into a local soft-rock station, I settled back and coasted on home – the commuter traffic thinning until I was on the 299 again.

Finally I parked at the top of my drive and walked down to the front door. There was a thin manila package propped against it. Elizabeth had been quicker than usual, which wasn't a good sign. I picked it up, unlocked the door, reset the alarm, and walked into the large, open plan living room.

The view through the sliding glass doors made me stop just to take it all in. The canyon, at my point, went from East-West. In the mornings it caught the sunrise, and at the end of the day the large glass panels would often frame impressive sunsets. Ever since moving in, I had been able to immerse myself in the colours and the textures of Mother Nature. Along the canyon sides, the sparse clumps of pine and shrub were home to a variety of wildlife, which helped to keep us Concretes entertained when the TV and radio reception got too bad and the phone lines were down.

Uncle Nathan had also loved nature, and designed the house to present the best views from all its levels.

Externally, the house had been constructed like a three-tiered wedding cake. Cut down the middle, half of it had been stuck onto the canyon wall 60 feet above the river. He'd thought about the position in regard to the changing shadow cast by the opposite canyon wall. That was why foot square pieces of armoured glass had been inserted into the living room roof, which doubled as the kitchen veranda. The same stolen light technique had been used on the kitchen roof, which also formed part of the third tier's open decking area.

Access to and from the house varied, depending on the dictates of the weather, as to which dirt tracks and paths you took. CalTrans ensured the roads were maintained to a high standard throughout the year, so Concrete annually helped out with the Adopt-A-Highway programme, by way of saying thank you.

The open plan living room sat at the front of the house, with two of the four bedrooms off to the sides towards the back. Up a dark wood staircase, the landing opened out to the kitchen at the front, plus two more bedrooms to the rear. Up again, and the third level was yet another large living area-cum-observation room.

The whole place had been built from natural materials found around the canyon itself. Cemented, locked and pinned into the canyon wall, it blended in with the background.

Both the house and the office had been my inheritance from Uncle Nathan. The office is mine, rent and utility free, for as long as I made use of it. After which Jack Orion – or, more likely, one of his descendants – could then do with it as they saw fit.

For the life of me, I don't remember Uncle Nathan, so I have no idea why he left me anything in his will. He never visited the family, or myself, while we were in England, but I didn't know what contact he'd kept when Mom finally left Dad for a new life in Paris. The trouble was, with him being close family, a regular DNA test wouldn't prove anything.

Which was saying I was able to find some of his DNA in the first place. I had my suspicions, but Dad had always treated me like his own son – even going out of his way to write to all the family about my success in getting a place at Sandhurst.

However, with repeated postings to Northern Ireland, the Gulf and the Balkans, our politics had diverged and further coloured our relationship over his final years.

But that was in the past – time to get back to the here and now.

The lack of food was finally getting to me, so I picked up the phone and ordered myself pizza.

Captain Chilli's Exploding Tomato Pizzeria – "Every pizza guaranteed to blow your head off!" – was run by a pair of extreme-sports fanatics, and although they appeared to be overly bohemian and laid back, they actually cared for their product. They were also the only place who would deliver for no extra charge.

Tossing Elizabeth's envelope onto the coffee table, I walked through the back and into the master bedroom. Stripping off, I hung the suit to one side for dry cleaning and tossed the laundry in the basket for a wash day, then spent ten minutes under a hot shower, trying to get the city out of my skin.

Drying myself off, I went back into the bedroom. Despite the evening's warmth the room felt cold and rejecting. The large double bed was still unmade, the cover and top sheet rucked up and pushed to one side, pillows still crumpled, two depressions still clearly visible.

I exhaled heavily, yanked open the wardrobe, and caught

sight of myself in the full length mirror fitted to the back of the door. I'd always tried to keep myself in shape, cared about my appearance, and exercised both body and mind whenever I had the chance. True, the jagged lightning bolt scar on my chest wasn't what I'd call attractive, but at least it was on the right hand side, and didn't look like bypass surgery performed by some crazed Dr. Frankenstein. And the rest of the chassis was in excellent shape as well, considering the mileage it had racked up over the years. Okay, so maybe there was a visible whiff of smoky grey in with the light brown hair, but so what? All the finest meat has been aged before being put out on display, and feeling good about yourself was really all that mattered.

Impulsively I pulled on a robe, grabbed some stuff off the rail and marched myself into the adjacent guest bedroom. Ten minutes later, with fresh linen on the bed and some personal effects on the nightstand, I figured it would do until I got my head back together.

As my spirits started to lift, I put on a pair of light slacks, an old RMA Sandhurst T-shirt, and a pair of flip-flops before going back into the warmth of the living room. I switched on the hi-fi and relaxed as the rich sounds of Concrete's own jazz-orientated Night Train flowed softly from the speakers. I poured a small Irish whiskey and nursed it as I looked out at the night sky. Experience had taught me there was no point in drinking to forget; you just end up forgetting to stop. Then you'd waste your time trying to remember what you'd successfully forgotten.

The sound of the delivery man knocking on the door indicated the arrival of pizza, and the smell from the Mutant

Margherita he handed over was sinfully seductive. As I paid the guy, I wondered how he'd made it over to the canyon. It wouldn't be the first time he'd been pulled over for speeding in a wind-powered land yacht. Not forgetting the time I had to lend a hand to pick bits of broken gyrocopter off the canyon wall.

*****

Later, with the pizza slowly dissolving my stomach lining, I lay on the long couch and went through a two minute relaxation routine. In a more receptive mood, I opened the envelope, and started to read Elizabeth's report.

I don't remember making it past the first half page.

3

I woke feeling cranky, despite the bright sunshine already starting to slide through the glass patio doors. The radio was still on: "You're tuned to Concrete's Community Radio! This is the Morning Coffee Show, and I'm Robbie Moore, the boy next door, letting you know the weather forecast for the city is hot and breezy. So don't forget to wear something thin and flimsy girls! Meanwhile, here's The Carmichael Brothers to tell you about their footwear fetish."

Glaring at the speakers, I carefully got up and started to work the stiffness out of my back and shoulders – not completely sure if the pain was from sleeping on the couch, or from the terrible pun on the song title.

"I'm a soul man...."

I shook my head. At the next Concrete Council meeting I was going to have to table a motion for getting "the boy next door" whacked and laid six feet under.

Picking Elizabeth's report off the floor, I cut through to the guest bedroom at the back, stripped off and stepped into the ensuite shower. It felt good just to let the hot water and a bar of Simple Sally soap work their magic. While still under the jets, I shaved with my eyes closed – an old Army time saving habit I've never been able to break.

I dried myself off, flossed, brushed, then dressed in khaki cotton pants, loafers and an open-necked polo shirt. I checked myself out in the wardrobe mirror. Maybe more Wal-Mart than Wall Street but, damn, I was surfing on a wave of happiness and actually feeling good about myself.

Closing the wardrobe door, I looked at the guest bed, and the grey clouds swept into my mind again. Wipe out. I wondered if it might do me good to move in here properly for a while, let my emotions calm down before venturing out into the waters once more. Plenty more… Yeah, right. Time to pick up the board and go looking for a tube to shoot.

Positive actions, positive thoughts. They say – whoever they might be – the best way to start the day is with breakfast, which was all the incentive I needed to climb the stairs to the kitchen. The morning sun was coming up over the trees and canyon rim, spreading a bright zone across the veranda decking and the hardwood kitchen floor. Can't beat a jolt of heart-warming sunshine for putting a smile on the lips of any good and honest creature. That's how you can tell the bad guys. They don't smile.

Nodding sagely to myself, I took some eggs and three links of sausage from the refrigerator. Dropping the sausages in a heavy fry pan, I left it on a medium flame while I broke the eggs into a bowl. A little salt, a little pepper… Pepper? Ah, now I knew what had been missing. Reaching over I pressed a button on the kitchen sound system. From the speakers came, not the expected sound of Art Pepper, but Miles Davies. One of his classic early albums, in the original mono mixes.

The sausage started to pop and spit, leaking a little pork fat, and I started to beat the eggs with a fork in time to Jimmy Cobb brushing the hi-hat. I was just about to take it to the bridge when the sausages began crying to be taken off the heat. Putting them on a plate, I poured the eggs in and stirred them around with the fork to keep them from sticking too much.

When they were done, I dished them up with the sausage, pulled a couple of paper towels from the wall dispenser for napkins, rolled back the patio door and went out onto the veranda. Off to one side I'd put a small, square, pinewood patio table and two simple wooden director's chairs. I slid the plate onto the table, then tucked the paper towels under its edge to stop them from getting away in the light breeze.

I walked over to the rail, found the garden twine I'd wrapped around it, and started to pull up the morning newspaper tied to the other end of the line. From behind I heard a slow, methodical, thump, thump, thump of something hard and heavy hitting against the wooden decking. Without turning around I said loudly, "Wait your turn!"

Unhurried, I freed the newspaper and tossed the weighted line back down again. Reading the front page, I went back to the table, picked up one of the sausages and flipped it across the decking. Some more thumping, then the sound of slobbering and chomping as the sausage was devoured by the

Richardsons' dog.

He was a big and old golden Lab who could usually be found lying on his side on the kitchen veranda decking. He wasn't part of the original inheritance as such – he was here when I moved in, so I just assumed he was kith and kin, so to speak.

It wasn't until I'd asked some of the other canyon residents about Uncle Nathan's Labrador, that my suspicions had been confirmed.

"Oh no, that's not his dog. That's the Richardsons' dog!"

Try as I might, I could find little or nothing about the elusive Richardsons, except that through no choice of my own, I now had their dog as a permanent house guest.

His short coat had a scattering of grey and white in amongst the gold and, given his nature, it was hardly surprising as he'd certainly seen some action in his time. He was missing a couple of toes, which didn't seem to affect his ability to come and go as he pleased, and while one eye had that slate grey cloudiness of an obvious cataract, the other was as clear and clean as a mountain spring. Years of practice meant he knew how to manipulate human pity and he was adept at squeezing the very last drops of sympathy from almost anyone. He even thinks it still works on me – but that's just because I don't have the heart to disillusion him.

The thumping of his tail on the decking slowed, then stopped as he stretched himself out, shuddered a little, broke wind in the key of C#, then settled down to sleep again.

He was also the reason why the newspaper got tied to the string.

Some time back, the paperboy used to ride out on his mountain bike and throw the rolled-up paper onto the kitchen veranda. On more than a few occasions, I'd caught him trying to hit the dog. I'd shout as he was cycling off, but it didn't seem to have any effect on the kid.

A few days after his last successful hit, I came out onto the veranda with a plate of breakfast, sat down, then heard a terrified voice calling out, "Mr. Rhimes? Can you call your dog off please?"

I strolled over to the railing and looked down. At the bottom of the driveway, the paperboy was using his bike as a defensive barrier. At the top of the drive, blocking the kid's exit, was one very pissed off Richardsons' dog. The dog's hackles were up, teeth bared, and even at this distance I could hear his angry growl. Maybe pissed off was an understatement.

Offhandedly I called down to the kid, "He's not my dog, kid. He's the Richardsons' dog."

I was tempted to say 'dawg', but resisted, on the grounds I wasn't smoking a corncob pipe or chewing on a plug of tobacco.

"Please, Mr. Rhimes! I promise I won't do nothing to tease him no more!"

"Won't do nothing no more is an extra-double negative, kid. Don't they teach you nothing at school?" Ah, Harry Rhimes, leading by example.

But the kid was obviously scared, and while tossing newspapers at dogs then trying to outrun them on a bike wasn't the smartest of moves, it was time to put an end to the situation.

I went back into the kitchen, took some twine out of a drawer, tied one end around the railing and threw the rest down to him.

"From now on just tie the paper to the end of this, okay?"

"Whatever you say, Mr. Rhimes. Just call the dog off!"

I turned my head a little and looked the Richardsons' dog in the eye – either the good or the bad one, I can't remember which – and shouted "Hey, Fuckwits, get in here now!"

The dog stopped growling, let his hackles down, and snorted contemptuously. Then he casually sauntered back along a trail and onto the kitchen veranda's edge, his tail swinging from side to side as if nothing was wrong.

For the record, he responds to, "Hey," rather than anything else – as in, "Hey! Nice dog!", or, "Hey! Who are you, old fella?!" Usually, though, it's, "Hey! If you're going to do that, do it downwind!" Let's face it, if I were to stand on the veranda and shout out "Hey, Fuckwits, get in here now!" every time I called the dog, I'd have half the town's human population showing up at my door in no time.

I settled back and finished my sausage and eggs, Miles still playing in the kitchen, and flicked through the newspaper. As usual, a lot of nothing, interspersed with coupons and adverts. Not surprising considering it was late in the year, and with the tourists thin on the ground it was up to the local inhabitants to keep the journalists' insatiable appetites for sleaze and scandal sated.

Time passed, the sun continued to climb, and it was around 9 a.m. when I finally set off for my appointment with the Llyle family. I'd changed into a white shirt, plain tie, and a charcoal grey cotton two-piece suit. All the better to make a good first impression. The Ford might not have had the best air conditioning, but it always paid to dress for the occasion, regardless of how warm the weather. For all I knew, the Llyles could become regular clients one day.

Driving out from the canyon wasn't so bad once you'd gotten used to the switchbacks, the summer dust, the occasional rock slide here and there, and the fact the hill climb grinds your transmission into an early grave. A 4 x 4, or maybe one of the new style pickup trucks, would handle the back roads far easier. Trouble was, it was too easy to spot such a vehicle, three or four cars back, when you were trying to tail someone. Whereas my old PoS, with its dusty windshield and tired paintwork, usually remained invisible to most drivers, even when close up.

Rounding the top of the canyon wall, it was just a case of cruising along the 299 until I'd skirted the city. From there, the highway climbed back up into Shasta County, and was easy cruising before I turned off onto the back roads once more.

As I drove along a parallel track road, I caught sight of the Llyle place. It was imposing and impressive, even from a distance. The architecture looked more like an official public building rather than someone's home, regardless of whom the someone happened to be. The front entrance was protected by a white painted, semi-circular, cement wall. To the rear, the grounds were protected by a double run of wire fencing. Add in foot patrols, along with camera surveillance, and it was doubtful the Llyles could ever be taken by surprise.

Following a signpost, I turned onto a length of sun-greyed tarmac driveway and coasted up at the front gates. They were large, wrought iron and wood constructions, which wouldn't have been out of place in a remake of Fort Apache or The Alamo. Along the top of the wall ran loops of razor wire like some kind of S&M slinky. Sunlight glinted from jagged shards of broken glass fixed into the top as an extra defence. Not so much a gated estate, more a case of heavily fortified.

To the right of the driveway was a 3 foot deep storm gully. To the left was a brick-and-wood shelter, which gave a rain and wind break to those who had to use the intercom.

Killing the engine, I got out and ducked into the shelter. On the back wall sat a brushed steel intercom with a pierced grill, a well-thumbed call button, and the protected eye of a miniature camera. Hmmmm. I'll be another five minutes, Mr. DeMille.

A laminated sign had been nailed up beside the intercom. In big black lettering were the words Buzz and Wait. So I buzzed, and waited.

There was a loud click, then the speaker hummed and crackled into life as a thin, metallic, male voice said, "State your name and your business."

I pushed the button. "Mr. Harry Rhimes. I'm here for a ten-thirty appointment with Mr. and Mrs. Llyle."

"Wait."

So I waited until the speaker hissed and crackled at me again.

"Okay, Mr. Rhimes, show the camera some ID."

I reached into my jacket pocket, withdrew my wallet and

flashed my driver's licence. Another bout of silence. In my mind's eye I pictured a bored security company guy. Dressed in a pseudo-military rent-a-cop uniform, I figured he was sitting in an operations centre up in the main house, finger-pecking the information into a computerised form.

From the speaker, the voice came back. "Everything seems to be in order. Mr. Steadman will be waiting for you up at the entrance to the main house. Er, you might want to back up a little though, before we open the gates. I take it your vehicle still has reverse gear?"

Ah, another loss to the entertainment industry.

I started the car and rolled several yards back down the driveway as the gates shuddered, then swung slowly outwards. Driving through left me in no doubt. This really was Fortress America.

The road leading to the main house curved out to the right before hooking back to the left in a crescent – more, I suspected, for effect than for any practical design. Seeing several other vehicles already in place, I parked to one side of a brick and flagstone carriageway which led to a short flight of stone steps and the main entrance. Fronted by ornate Doric columns and an impressive set of doors, the image and tone was of an 18th Century Governor's Residence, enhanced by an atmosphere which spoke of old money and older politics.

Another intercom greeted me at the door and a faint buzzing helped me locate the closed-circuit security camera as it rotated in my direction. Before I could do anything, the doors swung inward, revealing the hallway and, at a safe distance, the reception committee. It had consisted of a 30-something Hispanic security guard in a neat uniform, and to one side, a late middle aged man I took to be Mr. Steadman.

On one side of the guard's belt hung a matt black security wand, and the other side had an ugly, square-barrelled tazer within easy reach of a relaxed and steady hand. Steadman was impeccably turned out in a modern cut double-breasted suit, though there had been something about his stance and his body language which seemed at odds. If the reception committee was designed to impress, then it was certainly living up to expectations.

The guard stepped forward, took out the metal detector and proceeded to check for any concealed weapons. Although I'm licensed to carry, I didn't feel there was any need to this time. I mean, what sort of trouble could I get myself into just by asking about their son?

Once checked, the guard nodded an okay, then moved back to his safe spot, off to one side. Taking that as my cue, I smiled as warmly as I could before heading towards my escort, hand outstretched, ready for the initial shaking of – though as I approached he looked slightly perplexed and confused.

In a Southern fried accent he said, "Pardon my ignorance, sir, but am I right in the assumption you are a freelance journalist? Is there a camera bag? Recording equipment? Paraphernalia to be collected from your vehicle?"

Paraphernalia? Without even thinking about it I slipped into my best English. "I carry with me only the time-honoured tools of my trade, namely a notebook and pen. Now, lead on, dear boy, lead on!"

A look of pained resignation creased his face before being replaced by a mask of indifference. "If you would care to follow me, sir." He turned and pushed open another impressive set of doors which, in turn, opened out into a reception room.

Probably considered large in the real world, the room was decorated in tasteful opulence. Not so much as to say Gaudy, but enough to say Never Ever Been Strapped For Cash.

With the walls painted in sympathetic pastel colours, the room focussed on a sculpted Italian marble mantelpiece and surround, which framed a large cast iron fireplace. Above hung a massive mirror in an ornately carved and gilded frame which, on closer examination, confirmed its Pre-Independence Georgian roots. The drapes hung cinched over window shutters, which had been folded back to let in as much natural light as possible.

Halting in the middle of the room, Steadman turned to me. "If you would please wait here, sir. Mr. and Mrs. Llyle will be with you shortly."

He left, closing the doors behind him, leaving me wondering why a staff member would need an overly generous cut jacket and wear a button-sized transceiver almost totally concealed in his right ear. At least now his body language made more sense.

I took a slow walk around the room, pleasantly surprised at the way the early seventies Conran pieces blended in with more modern European designers. Several occasional tables were within easy reach, while along the far wall was a Japanese-influenced sideboard with an Art Nouveau Tantalus sitting on top.

The click of the door catch brought me back to the present.

Turning around I was first greeted by Mrs. Llyle, then Steadman again, pushing Mr. Llyle in his wheelchair.

I knew Roger Llyle was in his 70s, but his frailty still surprised me. Originally from a wealthy family, he'd made his money through a string of businesses, and lost a small fortune in alimony to his first wife in the process. The wheelchair was down to an accident he'd suffered on a sub-contractor's construction site. Despite the surgeon's best efforts the damage to his spine and neck had left him paralysed from the waist down. He sued the company for every penny they had, literally, and when the company was bankrupt, stepped in and bought it, lock, stock and Chapter Eleven barrel, for the sum of one dollar. Before he finally sold it on though, the company had been placed in the Wall Street 500.

Regardless of his power and status, sitting in the wheelchair he came across as atrophied, small and doll-like, in a French blue three-piece suit, white shirt, and a powder blue bow tie. His bald scalp and face was reminiscent of an early Boris Karloff, in the RKO version of The Mummy, and I guessed he had more wrinkles than an elephant's scrotum. Not that I'm readily conversant with elephants' scrotums, but I've seen enough issues of National Geographic to recognise one, even at a distance.

His fingers were thin and bony, attached to wrists and forearms which seemed swamped by the shirt and jacket cuffs – the frailty amplified by an overly large, loose fitting Rolex – while his fingers twitched and fluttered listlessly in his lap like two small birds squabbling over a crust of bread. Yet his clear, bright grey eyes, were youthful, quick and still full of sharp intelligence.

Margaret Llyle, on the other hand, was somewhat of an enigma. Despite good plastic surgery and regular hits of Botox, I knew she was mid-50s, if she was a day. From what I'd read in the social columns, she'd married Roger Llyle right after his divorce. So quickly, in fact, some people believed she had been waiting in the wings, with her bouquet and bridesmaids at the ready, even before the decree nisi had landed on the family lawyer's desk. Depending on whose social commentary you followed, she had either been a cocktail waitress, a lap dancer, or a personal services type of masseuse. Perhaps even all three. But whatever her past, it had been successfully buried from prying journalists. The one thing everyone seemed to agree on, however, was that she had married way above her station.

She stood around five-seven tall and had chosen to dress very Jackie Kennedy. It was a semi-formal two-piece in light salmon, which did her no favours. Her hair, having dyed a thousand deaths, had been lacquered to within an inch of reanimation. I wondered why she hadn't thought to employ a stylist, or some other professional to advise her. From her body language it was clear she felt self-conscious and uncomfortable.

Closing the doors behind him, Steadman wheeled Llyle closer to the chairs. I expected him to leave. Instead he took up a position directly behind Llyle, feet slightly apart, hands behind his back. Relaxed, yet attentive. I waited for Mrs. Llyle to settle herself before I sat down across from her.

Smiling, she broke the ice. "Out of interest, which magazine will your series be appearing in? There are so many these days that–"

The sound of Roger Llyle sighing stopped her mid-sentence.

"I don't think Mr. Rhimes is here to interview us for any proposed article, are you, sir?" He chuckled a little, which merged into a slight cough. "Mind you, I was taken with the title. The Great American Good. It has a ring of plausibility to it, I'll give you that." His expression told me not to push the cover, so I just held up my hands in surrender.

"You're right; I'm not a freelance journalist. I'm here to discuss a delicate and personal matter." Deliberately I looked towards Steadman standing behind Llyle's wheelchair.

Llyle nodded. "Don't worry about him. When it comes to family scandal, he's as deaf as they come. Isn't that right, Steadman?"

Steadman deigned not to answer.

Across from me, Margaret Llyle covered her embarrassment with an aggressive, cold anger. "Who the hell do you think you are, coming into this house and invading our privacy? Steadman call house security. I want this filth thrown out. How was he able to make an appointment in the first place? Roger, do something to stop him and his kind digging around all the time." Her face flushed, despite the colour of her make-up.

"No need to get upset, Margaret, Mr. Rhimes is here to talk about Preston, aren't you?" He looked over at me, a thin smile catching the corners of his mouth. "I didn't think Ms. Fairfax had it in her to hire someone, but I'm assuming she's your client? Otherwise there's no reason for her visiting you yesterday, is there?"

"Seems you're way ahead of the curve, and I apologise for any offence I might have caused." Sometimes a little humility pays back with dividends, and I could see no point in being confrontational. Nor in denying something Llyle had obviously checked up on, despite Daw's promise of anonymity.

Margaret sat back on the davenport and glowered at me.

With that avenue closed, I turned to Roger Llyle. "Ms. Fairfax hired me to find your son. Once I have that information, I'll pass it on to her. After that, it's up to her what she decides to do with it. As far as I can tell, she wants to ask him why they broke up. Beyond that, I've no other interest."

Again the thin smile danced at the edges of the old man's lips.

"That's gratifying to know, Mr. Rhimes. However, I fear you're on a wild goose chase. From what I understand, the two of them were romantically involved for a while – about a year and a half I believe?" He looked over to Margaret, but she remained silent. Turning his head to me, Llyle continued, "But, for whatever reasons, Preston felt it was not in their best interests to continue the relationship. Perhaps, in hindsight, he could have been more tactful and diplomatic about it, but it appears this young woman has taken his departure to heart. I believe Ms. Fairfax felt there was more to the relationship, yet to Preston it was more platonic than anything of a physical nature."

Margaret Llyle suddenly moved forward in her seat, the hem of her skirt riding up a little as she did so.

"She's not claiming she's pregnant by Preston, is she!? I

swear to God, as soon as it's safe to do so I'll have the little bastard DNA tested!" The look of raw hatred slowly faded as she made an effort to sit back again, trying to discretely adjust her skirt at the same time.

Roger Llyle waved a hand in her direction, obviously annoyed at the interruption, then looked inquiringly at me.

I tried to smile as I reassured her. "I believe she's not pregnant, if that will help ease some of the tension between the family and herself." I waited to see if Margaret would react, but her anger seemed deep and irreconcilable.

I shook my head a little. "I can appreciate the relationship came to an end and that it seems my client is not prepared to admit it's over, but…." I looked towards Roger again. "It might be best if Preston met with her and told her to her face."

Roger Llyle coughed out a short laugh. "They're hardly star-crossed lovers, Mr. Rhimes. I doubt very much there's anything to be gained from such a meeting. As it is, both Margaret and I have no idea where he might be. We have extensive grounds around this house alone, and that's before we start talking of holiday homes, cabin retreats, vacation sites…."

The vague movement of his jacket made me think he'd shrugged his shoulders. When I looked across at Margaret, I could have sworn she was gloating rather than smiling insincerely at me.

I smiled insincerely back. "So you've no objection to me asking around for information?"

Her grin compressed until her lips formed a thin red slash in her efforts to contain her anger. Roger sighed heavily. "If I can help with any questions you might have, then I will. But I insist this is the last time."

I nodded. "Seems fair to me. Can you tell me anything about this?"

From my jacket pocket I pulled out the copy of Lindsey's photograph. Steadman moved forward and carefully took hold of it, so Llyle could study it in detail.

"My word…. Well, I have to admit this is a few years old. About four or five I think…" He looked over to Margaret, but she pointedly refused to glance at the picture. Roger went back to studying it. "It must have been when he was involved with some sort of pro or college football business. The Greagson's eldest, Wesley, got him involved with something along those lines. Preston has always had a very strong interest in sports and athletics."

"Does he have any other girlfriends, ex-college sweethearts, cheerleaders?"

"You'd have thought so, but no, not that I can immediately recall. He's more focussed on competing and winning. He's always been very performance driven. At least, in some areas, that is. Can't say I know much about his personal relationships."

There are times when, no matter what you do with the dice, you always throw snake-eyes.

"In that case do you know if Preston is gay?"

The atmosphere in the reception room dropped from merely cold, down to frigid.

With a great amount of control Margaret Llyle half whispered, "You filth. Tell him to leave, Roger. Now. I want him gone. Now!"

Roger looked over to me. "I'm afraid Margaret is right, Mr. Rhimes. It's time for you to leave. Before you do though, to answer your question. Firstly, no. Preston has never shown any sign, or intimated such to either of us, that his orientation is anything other than heterosexual, regardless of how outwardly dysfunctional his private life may appear. Secondly, even if he were gay but not yet out to friends and family, it's still none of your business. And thirdly, Steadman will see you off the premises. Good day, sir."

I nodded my thanks to both of them, then followed the aide through into the entrance hallway again.

Unceremoniously he said "Farewell, sir," then handed me over to the guard. "Michael, once you've escorted Mr. Rhimes to his car, make sure you put his name on the Undesirables list."

Without giving me a second glance Steadman turned and headed back into the inner sanctum of the house.

Michael looked at me, shaking his head in sympathy. "Guess you've been a bad boy," he said as he walked me up to the main door and watched as I headed back to my car.

Extract from Catch a Falling Star
Kelly Lewis

Journal Entry Dated Wednesday May 7th 1975

I've always hated skin work. At least since I found out what it actually was, rather than what it wasn't. Which was why my boyhood dreams of becoming an internationally acclaimed porn star, had been dashed on the jagged rocks of despair. It was precisely two minutes after the manager of the Brunchy Burger Bar handed me the furry cat suit, and told me to stand outside and start enticing the punters in.

Back in digs yesterday, after nearly four weeks of long and depressing day shifts, I flopped down on the sofa and had a good moan.

"I tell you, Billy, not only is it embarrassing as hell, it's also very demeaning."

"And waving your dick at a camera lens isn't? Look, Michael, you're barely street legal as it is, so be thankful you're getting paid. It might not go towards your Equity card, but it'll go towards the rent at the end of the month."

Billy Canning had been 'resting' for as long as I'd known him. His last had been as one of thee people 'picked at random' who couldn't tell butter from some revoltingly strange stuff made from fermented Yak's milk. I was staying with him and some friends in an old three storey terraced house, which would've been converted into tiny bedsits, were it not for the renters' protected status. The landlords changed on a regular basis, and despite modernisation to the ground floor – which had been turned into several shop fronts housing an assortment of businesses over the years – the living areas still retained a sense of late 1950s early 1960s faded squalor.

Then the phone out in the hallway rang. It was Miriam – my agent – which was certainly an occasion for trumpets. She wanted to know if I would be available to do a short notice panto call, in some scout hut at the back of Ashley Street tube. I had to look it up in the A to Z while she was wibbling on.

"It's on account of someone having to drop out," she says, stating the obvious as if it were a totally new discovery.

"They weren't one half of a horse, were they?" After weeks in the cat suit I was in dire need of therapy, but there was little chance of that on the NHS! Miriam sounded confused, so no real change there.

"Would you rather play half of a panto horse?" Sound of her flicking through some papers on her desk. "There's nothing like that on the lists at the moment. Would a cow suit instead? They need one desperately in Reading – The Academy. It's not A-list casting, but if you think it would be a good fit?"

Give me strength! "No, dear, it's just if I'm part of a horse and I accidentally injure myself then they might be under contract to shoot me."

"What?" Her train of thought fought valiantly against being derailed, and despite my best efforts she successfully got us back on track. "The call's for a walk on in the second half. Ten lines. Twelve if you pad it."

Heaven forbid I'd upstage someone in panto. Oh yes you would! Oh no I wouldn't! Still, with the bad winter weather on the way it would be a damn sight better than being a freezing pussy out on the streets in December – ask any prostitute. So it was up at the crack of sparrow fart, pick a piece to memorise on the train, grab some toast and a couple of swigs of tea from the kitchen, then off on the Underground to Ashley Street.

Out of the station and into a bitterly cold North wind, and I'm half way down the street before I realise my nipples are like doorstops! Dolly Parton, eat your heart out! Of course, if I'd worn a vest as Billy had suggested then things wouldn't have been so obvious, but I've always felt that cotton vests were like Old Spice – given at Christmas to dirty old men, or your grandfather, which was pretty much the same thing in our house, as luck would have it.

When I finally got there the Scout & Community Hall wasn't too bad at first – sort of warm and inviting, like a middle-aged disreputable aunty – until I realised the smell from the extra paraffin heater and the creosoted walls was starting to jam the hell out of my sinuses. Wooden floor, wooden walls, wooden roof – even the wooden stage at the far end looked battle scarred and world weary. But I was determined not to let the atmosphere get me down, and on the positive side it looked like only five of us had tuned up for the call – all hopeful of getting to play the part of Third

Cowboy.

God knows who originally put it all together – let alone successfully pitched it – but the production was Robin Hood and the Nottingham Sheriff. Sheriff as in 'bang-bang shoot 'em up' Roy Rogers. "More hay, Trigger?" "No thanks, Roy. I'm well and truly stuffed!"

The other four were there already, sitting on folding wooden chairs placed in a line along the far wall, and all holding little cards with numbers on them. I went over to the trestle table in front of the stage, pick up the remaining card – number three – then took my place between two and four. Number one looked as if he was part of some Alamo re-enactment society, and for a moment I wondered if it might've helped if I'd also turned up in costume. Several minutes ticked by before someone else walks in, and settles themselves in front of an old upright piano half hidden in the corner, but I'm still concentrating on remembering the piece I've decided to read for this new development to impinge on my reality.

The jury of my peers, when they finally arrived and settled themselves, consisted of three nondescript people I didn't recognise (*later, Clive Shenny would go on to direct and produce The Waterfall Boys in 1979 for Granada, to great critical acclaim – then have total failures for the next ten years and end up committing suicide on New Years' Eve 1990*) and as we sat on the rickety wooden chairs, waiting our turn, I thought calming thoughts and tried to centre myself into the right frame of mind I thought a cowboy might have. The best I could come up with were black and white TV memories of The Lone Ranger, which then led to several minutes of self-conscious leg crossing while I desperately tried to think of someone more appropriate, who had not been a schoolboy crush.

What dragged me back into the realms of reality, was when I heard one of the casting committee say to the hopeful dressed as Davy Crockett, "Now if you could just select a song from the top of the piano, we'd like to hear you sing."

Sweet John Julius Norwich! Sing? Miriam never said a thing about having to bloody sing!

As the first two went through their paces I could feel my throat tightening up, little by little – not helped by the second bloke handing the pianist some sheet music he'd brought along for the occasion. Then I'm called to read. I do my best to sound manly and convincing, but with my tight throat and nerves I end up sounding like Tim Curry on helium, and knowing I've totally lost it I finish by doing several chunks of Romeo & Juliet on amphetamines: "Do-you-bite-your-thumb-at-me-sir? Who-sir? Me-sir? Yes-sir-you-sir-do-you-bite-your-thumb-at-me?"

There's a deafening stunned silence when I finally stop, then one of the three asks me to step over to the piano. As I start to shuffle through the sheets, the old boy at the upright smiles and whispers, "You're doing great, son. Who's your favourite singer?"

"Carmen Miranda," I say, not realising he's trying to throw me a much needed lifeline.

"Well, that's both of us fucked then." He smiles, then hands me something instantly forgettable, and I have to hold it up close to read it, which helps to cover my tone deaf rendition.

Out on the cold street again, I scurry around trying to find a phone box, then try to find one that hasn't been converted into some kind of Turner Prize entry. Local call to Miriam, so tupp'ences at the ready in case the ten pence piece isn't enough.

"How did it go?" she asks.

"Don't ask me to relive it all, otherwise I'll never come out of therapy," I tell her, desperately trying to forget the helium voice still in my ears.

"That bad?"

"Worse! They asked me to sing!"

"Oh…." There's a short pause, then she adds a little sheepishly, "Didn't I mention that when we talked about it?"

My anguished cry of frustrated rage is met by someone knocking on the telephone box door. "Are you finished in there, mate?"

"No! Now piss off!"

In my ear I hear Miriam saying, "Got to go, got another client waiting. I'll give you a ring if you get a call back." And then she's gone, leaving the machine to swallow my ten pence piece as I slam the receiver down.

I barge out of the box as several onlookers stare at me. The guy who knocked before suddenly pipes up, "You haven't broken it, have you?"

I resist the urge to turn on him. It's too cold and the post-failure depression is starting to bite just as deeply as the midday wind. Once home I treat myself to a large mug of hot chocolate with a generous splash of rum in it, then settle down for a serious slab of afternoon telly. Crown Court, followed a

little later by the consummate professionalism that is
Crossroads.

67

Extract from Twist of Vengeance
Alice Rothwell

1

"George?" Dickey Bellman stuck his head round the oak panelled office door without knocking. "Just heard the news from one of the couriers. Is it true?"

He stepped uninvited into George Effinger's office, sat down in the armchair by the window, and quickly lit up a Turkish cigarette. Wreathed in tobacco smoke, his expression was as expectant as a child's at Christmas as he waited for George to answer.

"'Fraid so, Dickey. I've already spoken to Arthur Gryffen about it, and he's provisionally accepted my resignation. I expect I'll be composing a proper letter this evening. Probably get one of the couriers to collect it from my flat tomorrow morning. That way the partners and the rest of you won't be too disrupted." He sighed, still a touch downhearted. "I've nothing outstanding after this afternoon's fiasco, what with the Bradley trial having finally reached its predictable conclusion. That was the only thing I had left to complete. A little prophetic don't you think? If you're into portents and signs, that is."

In reality, it'd been the summing up, before breaking for lunch, that'd decided it for him. That, along with the scratchings and mutterings coming from the gallery as the hacks shorthanded Judge Carmichael's address to the jury. Towards the end, he'd even lost the incentive to object to the Judge's unsubtle guidance, or the obvious indifference Carmichael had shown to the plight of the defendant. In many respects he'd known, deep down, that it was going to be a pre-ordained conclusion, based on the grounds of what was, to even the most impartial of observers, blatantly manufactured evidence.

True, his client, Raymond Bradley, had up to then been a particularly malodorous piece of work, and was undeniably guilty of more than a lifetime of crime throughout the whole of his twenty-six years of existence. But on this particular occasion he was, for once, actually innocent, and despite George's best efforts, he hadn't been able to prove it. Or at the least, not within reasonable doubt in the case of the jury.

However, as Scotland Yard's sage-like Inspector Hollywell pointed out to him, in the snug of the Three Ferrets – a public house almost equidistant between the courts and the offices of Maplethorpe, Bartlemass and Gryffen – it had been much more than just "a bit of a done deal."

"Between you and me, Mr. E, take it with a lick of treacle and be done with it. Because you'll not get another forensic quack to say it's an assumption and not a fact. Tighter than two sailors in a hammock those Home Office lot, believe-you-me."

George had taken a calming sip of whiskey before replying. "If the Judge had any sense, then he would've questioned the late arrival of such incriminating evidence. Especially as your constables stated – under oath, I might add – they'd previously searched Bradley's accommodation, and came up empty handed the first time round. Anyone with a bottle of Indian ink can forge a laundry mark and fade it with a bar of carbolic."

"But Micklethwaite's unusual AB blood group all over the shirt, and on the handle of that fancy French cutthroat razor, is another matter entirely. No, Mr. E, I'm afraid Bradley's been getting away with far too much, far too often, and various powers that be have a desire to see him detained at His Majesty's, regardless of your best efforts. Mind you, could be worse. At least the bugger's not going to swing."

The jury didn't take long, and they'd returned almost immediately after lunch. The foreman had barely given a perfunctory "Guilty!" before Judge Carmichael's declaration of "Fifteen years!" followed close on its tails. With most of the warm and sunny afternoon remaining, the court was cleared within five minutes, leaving George Effinger almost alone, and at the start of what others in the more established professional religions tended to call, A Question of Faith.

The walk back to MB&G had been contemplatively introspective, the spring weather making him realise just how much time he'd spent cooped up in offices and courtrooms since successfully passing his exams. Add to the equation the fact he was only a year older than Raymond Bradley, and a cold blanket of depression seemed to wrap itself around him all the more.

Dickey opened a window, flicked his cigarette end out onto the lawn below, and closed it again. "But what are you going to do, George? I mean, if I were to resign tomorrow, father would go bonkers and mother would start trying to marry me off again." He sounded a little crestfallen at the way his life seemed to be totally beyond his own control. "You're lucky. You only have your Aunt to displease – and for the life of me I can't see how you'll ever be able to do that."

Behind his desk, George smiled at the mention of his ex-guardian, now in her late "never-you-mind, dear!" Both his parents had been killed in Monte Carlo, in the April of 1914, just before the start of the Great War. He'd been nine, still at boarding school, and he'd never forgotten the fateful evening when Aunt Celia Margaret had arrived on the doorstep of Larchman College. She'd terrified his formidable Housemaster, and told George to "Only pack anything of a sentimental value. You'll be staying with me from now on." It'd been the start of a unique chapter in his life, and one which hadn't quite come to a close just yet. Leastwise not if he wanted to get away from it all, and needed somewhere to stay for a while.

Effinger sighed again. "I suspect I'll spend a couple of days with her down in Brighton, before I make any decision as to what I'm going to do next. I've still no idea myself – except that I'm sure it'll have absolutely nothing to do with the legal profession. I've taken more than enough to realise that I need to find something which…." He paused a moment as he tried to express what he'd recently come to realise. "Something which is more self-fulfilling."

Dickey seemed a little non-plus. "You've not been reading any of those Russian books, have you? Old Maplethorpe said I should read some, so I could at least understand the enemy, as he put it. Though I've got to admit, they seemed pretty incomprehensible when you think about the recent market crash."

"Which is why I don't intend to start playing with stocks and shares myself. There has to be something else I can successfully turn my hand to, and I'm always open to suggestions." He looked inquisitively at Dickey, watching as Bellman's forehead creased in thought.

"Perhaps if you were to sleep on it, George, rather than making a rash decision? I mean, you haven't actually tendered any letter of resignation yet, have you. So no one would blame you if you just apologised to poor old Arthur. Tell him it was all a practical joke that went horribly wrong. Take a few days off, then come back and start on a fresh assignment. That should take your mind off things."

Effinger shook his head. "No, Dickey. If anything, I feel as though my mind is already off things. Stagnating, in fact."

"Are you sure? Maybe if you were to spend the night at the club it might change your mind."

George smiled. "I doubt anything is likely to change my mind, Dickey. Epiphanies are like that."

There was a knock on the half open door and Effinger called out, "Come in, Mr. Peterford."

The head clerk stepped into the room, but respectfully remained by the door. Six foot six and pencil thin, he had always looked to Effinger as if he would have been more at home running a funeral parlour.

"Sorry to bother you, sir, but do you have any idea as to when you'll be leaving? Only I'd like to get two of the junior clerks to start boxing up your things." He looked pointedly at his watch. "And it is getting on a little bit."

"Signs and portents, Dickey," Effinger said, good naturedly. "They can't wait to get rid of me!"

*****

The cab ride back to his apartment in Brampton Square had been uneventful, and he'd started to flick through the pages of the Evening News almost as soon as he'd settled in the back. While the taxi driver kept up a steady stream of commentary, which had been easy to ignore, he'd read about the American Democrats and Franklin D. Roosevelt's New Deal platform. If he'd been a gambling man, then he would've probably put money on the Democrats to win the upcoming November elections, despite the Republicans previously strong track record.

But as he walked through the oak and glass entrance to Denton House, Wilson – the night doorman – had politely stopped him.

"Good evening, sir. If you have a moment, I believe there is a letter for you to collect. Arrived in this evening's delivery."

Even if it hadn't been addressed in her particular shade of dark lavender ink, he would've recognised his niece's penmanship regardless. Automatically he ran the envelope firmly through his fingers. Feeling the folded card it obviously contained, his smile disappeared and his shoulders sagged a little.

Surprised by the change, Wilson asked politely, "Bad news, sir?"

George shook his head, "No. It's worse than that."

Before Wilson had a chance to enquire further, George had taken the lift up to his rooms on the third floor, leaving a decidedly confused doorman in his wake.

Once through the front door, he'd tossed his overcoat and the unopened letter onto the hall stand, before heading into the lounge, making straight for the cocktail cabinet, and the telephone on top of it. Waiting for the operator to connect him, he contemplated something alcoholic, and was partway through measuring gin for a gimlet when the woman came back on the line again.

"Just connecting you now, sir."

George put down the bottle and turned his attention to the conversation at hand.

"Hello, Aunt Celia."

"Oh dear. Do I detect from your tone of voice that Charlotte has sent you an invitation to Dashambly Hall?" Celia Margaret's accent still maintained its fashionable hint of Los Angeles, even thought she'd returned to England at the end of 1929. She'd managed to escape the worst of the Wall Street Crash by listening to several very astute market analysts, though it'd taken her several years and some artwork sales before she felt she'd fully recovered and was financially affluent once more.

Effinger still maintained his cool tone. "Why should she invite me for the weekend, when she knows full well I'm more than likely to be bored senseless by it all?"

Down in Brighton, Celia Margaret single-handedly pushed a cigarette into her ebony and gold holder, lit it, then exhaled before answering.

"I think it might have something to do with the War, dear. There's still a shortage of eligible young men, and even some of those have tastes for pursuits other than the opposite sex. And anyway, it would do you good to socialise. You're spending far too much time in London, and I certainly didn't bring you up for you to just bury yourself away again."

"But," George picked up the phone and sat down, putting the instrument on a nearby side table – the gimlet totally abandoned for the moment. "You know I don't see eye to eye with old Montague. His politics are so Edwardian, and as for his stand on Indian independence and Gandhi? We couldn't be further divided if we tried! I can't for the life of me fathom what it is that Charlotte sees in him."

"I don't know what she sees in him either, which is all the more indication that love is blind, I suppose. Whatever, she's sent you an invitation so the least you can do is send her a reply accepting it. It would probably do you good to get out of London for the weekend anyway."

George grinned a little wryly to himself. "It's likely to be longer than that. I've resigned; as of this afternoon."

"Well, you know I was never happy with you making a go of that particular profession – though at least you're still young enough to change your spots."

He'd initially headed down the barrister path because he'd originally felt he could stop injustice and protect the innocent. Sadly it'd taken only a short time for him to discover it was just as bad as any other business.

Before he could say anything more, Celia Margaret continued, "Go to Dashambly Hall and enjoy Charlotte's weekend thingy. Then come down to see me and we can talk things over after you've settled. I'll tell Marshall to get the guest room ready for Monday, or do you have other plans?"

Effinger paused and reflexively wrinkled his nose. "I know it'll be hell, but I suppose I might as well."

"Don't be so theatrical, dear. Brighton isn't that bad."

"I was talking about Dashambly Hall, not Brighton. Not everything's about you, Aunt Celia."

"Sadly not, dear. Sadly not."

2

The following morning he called Jenkin's Garage, and Andrew Colshaw, the chief mechanic, picked up the call on the second ring.

"Jenkin and sons, mechanical repairs and garage service."

"Andy, it's George Effinger. It's a bit of short notice, but can you fuel up my Riley Six? I'm going to be out and about for a week at least, so if you could also top up the spare cans as well, it'd be much appreciate."

"Going anywhere nice, sir?"

Effinger did nothing to disguise his feelings about the upcoming venture. "Country for the weekend, then down to Brighton."

"If you don't mind me saying so, sir, it sounds like you're not really looking forward to it."

"You can shoot outlaws, Andy, but you're stuck with in-laws."

"You can shoot them as well, sir. Only the law doesn't approve of it when you do. I'll get one of the apprentices to deliver the Riley to you before ten at the latest."

And true to his word, at 9:55, the doorman had rang to say the Riley Six was parked out front, ready for collection.

The journey cross country had felt good once he'd disentangled himself from London's grip, and despite stopping off for a spot of lunch, he'd made good time, arriving at the Dashambly estate just on 3pm.

As he drove up to the main hall, from a distance it all looked pretty imposing, almost regimental in its symmetric design and neatness. But the closer he got the more he could see the tiredness of the frontage, the roofing slates askew or slipped from worn out nails, the odd cracked pane of glass and the crumbling window sills.

Hard times indeed, and he felt grateful that his family didn't have any country seats or medieval mansions to devour any monetary inheritance. He had some money in a trust fund set up by his late parents, but it wasn't enough to totally abandon employment of some kind entirely. The death duties on the estate must have been crippling, and that was before taking into account the day to day running costs of the Hall and its staff.

Bringing the car around the front of the Hall, he parked down the side of the house where the old stables, garage, and generator house were located, surveying the other vehicles parked up before walking back to the front of the house.

The door to the main entrance was already ajar, and even before Effinger's eyes fully adjusted to the change of light, the loudly bellowed question caught him off guard.

"Where the hell did you spring from?! Well we've no more room in the guest wing, that's for sure!"

Red faced, and cheeks in full whisker, Major Montague Tendle Rushington-Hydes glowered at him as Effinger stepped over the threshold and into the cool, high ceilinged reception area.

From the stairway off to George's right came the sound of Charlotte's "Who's that? And Monty, stop being such a grumpus! It's not my fault there's a hole in the roof, is it."

To George, the Major said, "You're going to have to bunk up in one of the back bedrooms." Then, to the still invisible Charlotte, he called out, "I hope this is the last of your infernal menagerie to turn up? Regardless, I shall be in my study, away from all this chaos."

"I honestly don't know what's gotten into you of late, Monty, I really don't!" Charlotte Rushington-Hydes finally appeared at the top of the main staircase, then ran lightly down the stairs to greet George. Dressed in a just-out-of-fashion floral cotton summer frock and wearing light brown sensible shoes, her blonde hair was finger-waved and held in place by a small army of bobby pins.

"George! It's so good to see you again!" She stopped an inch away and double air-kissed, Hollywood style, before taking his hand and pulling him across the entrance hall and towards the breakfast-cum-morning room. In a slightly loud voice she intoned, "Don't worry about Major Misery, he doesn't really mean it."

Behind him, George thought he heard an "I'm afraid I damn-well do!" but it was lost as the Major beat a purposeful retreat back down the passageway and the sanctuary of his study.

Throwing the door wide, she breezed and chattered into the room, her feet silent on the dark blue carpet. The main table and sideboard had been cleared of breakfast things, and various newspapers were laid out on several occasional tables. The long curtains had been fully drawn so as to allow as much light in as possible as the sun moved over to the other side of the Hall, in preparation for the ritual of afternoon tea.

Having paused to take a breath, Charlotte said, "One of the stable boys will collect your bags and take them up to your room. Sorry you've been relegated to the old servants' quarters, only there's been another problem with the roof. One of the chimney pots came down last week, and the wretched thing's been leaking ever since. Not only do I have to contend with that, but there's yet more bad blood between Monty and his younger brother, Clive."

"Yet more? I thought they were destined to be forever in a state of constant antagonism? What's it about this time?"

Charlotte dropped down into a dark brown wingback chair set in the recess of the bay window. Sitting on the edge, she looked up at George and grimaced slightly. "It's what it's always been about. Whose things belong to whom. This time it's over the infernal will, with all its codicils and covenants and Lord knows what else. Clive has been desperate to reclaim his possessions for some time, but Monty seems to change his inventory list every six months, which means Clive has to check through all the new paperwork again, then sign it, then countersign it. Then there's the state of disrepair that Monty's let the Hall fall into. Clive is worried that some of the family's assets are in danger of being lost because of Monty's stubbornness and negligence."

"So they're still contesting over who owns what?" Charlotte nodded and looked at her hands while George shook his head slightly. "It's always a fine line in Law when it comes down to goods and chattels that offspring and siblings bring into the family estate. Sometimes I think it would be best if every item someone buys has a name tag on it. That would certainly help avoid confusion – but maybe not the acrimonious emotions."

Charlotte sighed. "All I know is that Monty derives some kind of perverse pleasure out of the whole business, even though he seems Hell bent on having the old place fall down around our ears. And the thought of actually selling Dashambly to Clive will never be an option. Well, not while Monty's still able to draw breath."

She laid her hands firmly on the chair rests and pushed herself further back into the chair, then brushed imaginary strands of blond hair away from her left ear with her fingers. It was an idiosyncrasy she had whenever she felt stressed or frustrated. "Besides the chimney and the roof, something much more ghastly has happened, which has really upset Monty."

"Aha!" George placed his hat on the coffee table, unbuttoned his driving coat, and sat in the over-sprung chair opposite Charlotte. "They've finally found his real birth certificate?"

Charlotte grinned good-naturedly. "It's worse than that. It's Michael."

"He's not been hauled up before the local magistrate for his driving again, has he?"

Charlotte's hand went back up to her forehead for a moment. "No, nothing so mundane. He's engaged to be married. Well, at least that's what he told me in our last telephone conversation."

George cocked his head to one side a little. "Clippy? Usherette? Someone from the typing pool? Which is it this time, I wonder?"

"I won't tease; she's a professional artiste. International cabaret, I think he said."

George pursed his lips. "That's sometimes smoking room talk for an exotic dancer." He leaned forward, conspiratorially. "She doesn't perform with a snake, does she?"

Charlotte's cheeks flushed a little. "What? Oh. Er, I –" Then she caught his smile. "Oh, honestly! You're incorrigible! Still, whoever she is, she's definitely not English. Spanish, I believe. Or Portuguese? I think that's what Michael said. And he's bringing her here to spend the weekend with all of us."

"Well, that's guaranteed to send Monty totally barking! Do you know anything more about her? Her name, perhaps? That can sometimes give a clue as to her nationality."

Charlotte settled into the subject. "Her name's Rosita Consuela Montoya. Sounds like one of those made-up film star names, doesn't it? Not that I get much chance to go to the cinema these days. Anyway, Montague immediately went off on one the moment I told him. I knew he would, so I left it until after we'd finished breakfast Wednesday morning. He's been dreadful over it ever since. You see, Michael took to confiding in me years ago, when Monty started to ignore him and favour Reggie. Then, last week, during a telephone conversation, Michael asked me in several roundabout ways to pass on the news to Monty. From what I could glean from the poor boy's conversation, it's obvious that he's pretty well besotted with this woman. He seems to think all Monty has to do is take one look at her when they arrive, and all will be well. But as soon as Montague found out he kept going on about how Michael was forever hiding behind my skirts – as he put it – which isn't true at all."

Effinger steepled his fingers and put them under his chin. "Oh Charlotte. You were never cut out for the wicked stepmother role, were you? Is that what the old boy meant when he said something about your menagerie?"

"Probably, possibly – I'm really not sure anymore. Anyway they're not all my guests. He's conveniently forgotten he was the one who originally invited the Cranfields – well, Patricia, mostly – because now he'd prefer it if they were elsewhere when Michael arrives with this woman."

George sighed, then asked patiently, "And who, pray tell, are the Cranfields? Are they people I should know?"

Charlotte wrinkled her nose. "If you'd been introduced then you'd certainly have remembered them. Monty and I first met them at Baily Pargeter's two – or was it three Christmases ago? Montague had been in a terrible mood the whole journey down. Then, after we'd settled into our room, Patricia Cranfield knocks on the door, cigarette in hand, and asks Monty for a light as she couldn't find any matches in their room. I can still remember it because the distinctive smell of her French cigarettes was quite pungent. I didn't think much of it at the time. But during the weekend she and Monty seemed to take to each other. I just put it down to the festive season and the fact that Baily Pargeter's never been one to be frugal with his wines and spirits.

"But then last Easter, out of the blue, Patricia and Jonathan turn up at our door, supposedly unannounced. Thankfully there was still some space to cater for them, but I found out later that Monty had been keeping in touch, and had invited them down himself. Well, her – mainly because he was a bit annoyed that Jonathan had come along as well. Almost from the start of that weekend the two of them kept flirting with each other – quite outrageously sometimes. It was a side of Monty I've never ever seen before, or at least never really openly acknowledged, and I have to say, Georgie, that I'm not really all that comfortable with the way the whole business is turning out."

"That doesn't really tell me much about them, does it."

Charlotte became a little cautious. "They're brother and sister – a Kent or Sussex family I think. Jonathan has obviously been banged about by the War. Tremors and nightmares, if friends are to be believed. I'm not entirely sure where he said he'd seen action, but he seems old before his time. I can understand how war can do that to a person."

"And the scarlet woman?"

"Patricia, is something of a modernist person, often fashionably daring, though sometimes she strikes me as being quite calculating…." Her voice trailed off for a moment, then, "I know that it's all totally harmless and purely for their own amusement – which is probably the only reason why Monty invited them here in the first place."

George looked down at his hands for a moment. "I don't want to seem judgemental – this is the Twentieth century after all – but it does seem a touch rum all the same."

Her hand brushed at her ear again. "He really doesn't mean anything by it. It's nothing more than a passing phase, and if it keeps him in good humour then I'm willing to turn a blind eye to the whole business."

"As long as you're prepared to tolerate it then I won't judge." To change the subject he asked, "Anyone else arrived yet, apart from the Cranfields?"

"Reggie. He arrived earlier this afternoon, just in time for lunch. Look, I know what you're going to say, but–"

"But if I'd known you'd invited that little weasel then I would've certainly declined the weekend. Why has he decided to grace us with his presence this time? Let me take an educated guess; he's already tried to clip either you – or more likely Monty – for enough money to help clear some of his debts?" Effinger held up a hand, silencing her before she could reply. "No, don't tell me – the less I know, the more I like it on that score. Who else did you invite? Fiona Collingwood, perhaps?"

"I sent a card, but she's never been one to RSVP. If she arrives unannounced then God knows where we'll put her up. Plus it'll mean an odd number for dinner. Why do you ask?"

Effinger feigned disinterest. "No particular reason – just that I've not seen her in a while, that's all."

Charlotte chose, for the moment at least, not to enquire further. "Mrs. Ackerman will also be joining us this evening. She's had a standing invitation since she arrived in the village, though I'm quite sure the two of you haven't met. She's also wonderfully batty and I know you'll just love her when you're introduced, so I won't spoil things. I've put the two of you together for dinner as I think you'll get on perfectly."

She paused for a second before carrying on. "Then, to help keep things varied, I've also invited the Reverend Hamblside and his wife, Melissa. He can be a touch too evangelical at times – Monty isn't a fan, calling them 'sanctimonious God bothers', but he will tolerate them on social occasions. The two of them moved up from London, but I'll let them tell you all about themselves – mainly as it may just prove to be a good diversion from the ruckus that Michael and this woman are likely to cause."

George did a quick mental calculation in his head. "If Fiona is going to be the odd one out, I think you're missing someone, aren't you? So far I've only counted twelve."

Charlotte blushed slightly. "The only other person I'm expecting to arrive soon is Donna Fairchild. Her telegram said she should be arriving probably around tea time."

George tried hard not to sound judgemental. "Oh."

Charlotte stood up out of the chair. "There's no earthly reason why she shouldn't visit now and again, is there? She's one of the few friends I have left from before I married Monty. Anyway, I doubt she'll be staying in the country long because I understand she has several writing projects lined up, now that she's become a successful authoress. Somewhere in America again. Hollywood, no doubt. She said she might be working with other women writers such as Lenore Coffee and Mary Pickford. Whatever it is, she's positive it's going to be a long term thing. Probably for five or six years, or even more if she has a box office hit. She's only stopping to say her goodbyes before she leaves." Charlotte paused when she realised how protective she'd become.

George said gently, "I didn't say she shouldn't be here, did I?"

"No." Then, defensively, she added, "But then I know what most people think of progressive women these days." She half smiled. "Heavens, what must you think of me?"

He smiled. "I think you can sometimes be an utterly naïve little innocent, filled with every good intention and no forethought as to the consequences. Always have, you know that."

Charlotte tried to hold firm, but then sat back down onto the padded brown leather seat, shoulders sagging. "Oh, Georgie." Effinger winced at the nickname, but said nothing as she continued, sounding a little dejected. "You have no idea what it's like being married to a man like Monty. How could you?" She carried on, her words coming in a rush of confused emotions. "It's just sometimes I find myself wondering just what it would be like to step down that path myself. I…." Her voice trailed off wistfully for a moment, before she got herself back under control. "We might have once been boarding school friends, but is it really that wrong for us to see each other from time to time? And, of late, Monty seems to get angry at the slightest of things, which is why I invited Donna, if only for the respite she provides while she's here."

George sat back as best he could in the confines of the wingback chair. "Monty had a reputation for being cantankerous and stubborn long before you married him. It was common knowledge in most circles." Then, with more concern in his voice, "He's not becoming violent towards you, is he?"

Charlotte looked a little shocked. "What? No, nothing like that." George waited while she composed herself again, letting her carry on. "I suppose he's no worse than when I married him, but I think it might well be more down to me than him this time. I've been so jumpy and on edge ever since I got to hear about Michael's impending visit. More so after I explained about his intentions to marry." She sighed heavily and looked down at her hands. "There have been occasions in the past when some people have said I should be more prepared – more capable, even – of standing up to Monty whenever his temper takes control, or even when he's in full bluster. But I know, deep down, I'm not that kind of person at all."

George tried to be tactful. "But still, you did agree to marry him all the same, and against the advice of others. Myself included."

"Yes!" Again she paused to get her emotions back under control. "Yes, I did. But, at the time, I thought he would calm down, once we were married. Or, at least, I thought I could be the one to calm him."

"Beauty and the Beast?" George shook his head. "Charlotte, we both know his first wife had the courage to walk out on him, and you don't do that without some good reason. Even in these emancipated times."

"As I understood it, she ran off with another man – so it might not have been all down to Monty's precarious moods." She paused while one of the two teenage stable boys knocked on the open door. Beside him were Effinger's two suitcases.

Charlotte looked up, then said, "Peter, you need to take them up to Cook's old room. Don't use the kitchen stairs, just go straight up."

The young man was clearly ill at easy in the unfamiliar surroundings. "Do you want me to unpack 'em for you, sir?"

George shook his head. "No, thanks, I can see to that myself."

As the sound of his feet disappeared up the main staircase, Charlotte looked imploringly at George. "Sometimes I honestly believe I made a silly mistake in marrying him. Then he'll be all charming and so attentive, which makes me forgive him everything – even though I also know Monty will probably never change, no matter what. I realise now that I should have listened to my father at the time."

Seeing an easy way out of the present topic, George asked, "And how is your father these days? I haven't heard from him in a while."

Charlotte brightened at the change of conversation. "He's apparently gone off South America – supposedly full of crooks and swindlers – and has totally given up on the Church of the Sacred Pipette. When last he wrote, he was staying at some clinic in California. It's run by a Doctor Theodophilous Q. Jacksonhammer. He's an exponent of the Kellogg Mind and Body Philosophy. Apparently, it involves lots of regular exercise, healthy eating, and doing unspeakable things with natural yoghurt and a hand pump. From the illustration it looks similar to the sort the gardeners use to spray the roses for greenfly. He enclosed something in his last missive called The Illustrated New Life Manual. I'll show you if you like?"

"I think I'll gracefully decline the pleasure. However, I know he's stubborn when he gets behind an idea – just as you were when it came to marrying Montague. But if you want to make something more of your life, then I suggest you pull yourself together first."

She smiled rather wanly. "I'll try, Georgie." She wrinkled her nose again, slightly embarrassed. "So, tell me: having made my bed, now I've got to lie on it, regardless."

"Ah, I doubt very much if anyone could comfortably lie on the bed you've made for yourself at the moment – even if they were as adept as an Indian fakir used to a bed of nails. Why don't you just cut your losses and jump ship?"

Charlotte smiled again. If there was one thing positively guaranteed to provoke a reaction from a dedicated Army man, such as Montague Tendle Rushington-Hydes, it was the use of Naval expressions in or near his presence.

"Because I just couldn't."

"Why ever not? You're still able to turn a gentleman's head. In fact, who was it who showed an interest in you at the last May Ball here?" He snapped his fingers a couple of times, then smiled. "Simon Jarvis; runs an oriental import and export business, as I recall. In fact, if I remember the occasion rightly, he would probably be more than willing to make a dishonest woman of you."

Charlotte blushed at the memory. "What a wicked thing to say! Though I must admit he was rather dashing, and difficult to ignore." Then she let her shoulders sag in resignation. "But I just couldn't do something like that. Nor what Monty and Patricia do in public, either. You, of all people, with your legal training and court experience – you know what happens in situations like that. I would just die of shame at the scandal, the newspapers would publish all the details, and I could never face the public scrutiny of the Divorce Court. And then there would be all that social gossip and insinuation afterwards."

George held up both hands in appeasement. "I'm just saying that you're still young enough, and pretty enough, to start over again. Provided you have the courage to do so. If ever you do, I can always put you in touch with several good, and very discrete, lawyers who specialise in that sort of thing. The days of you becoming part of Monty's goods and chattels the moment you married him are now long gone, thankfully."

He looked at his wristwatch. "Anyway, I thought you said Donna was arriving for tea?"

Charlotte looked at the ormolu clock on the sideboard and suddenly jumped up out of the chair.

"Oh my good heavens it's past four already! I must fly, or Monty will have kittens! Well, you know what he's like for routines and punctuality. Do you want to change and join us, or unpack first?"

"I could be ready in five minutes. But I think I'll dawdle with my unpacking and spin it out to twenty or so, just to ensure Monty's getting full value from his blood pressure medicine."

Charlotte went across and pulled him out of the chair. "Not only wicked, but beastly with it! And I love you all the more for it." She hugged him tightly for a moment, then darted off, leaving him to make his way up to the old servants' rooms, unpack and freshen up a little before heading down to the back lawn, precisely twenty-five minutes later.

3

As George exited the house through the drawing room French windows, briskly walking across the wide flag-stoned terrace and down the steps to the carefully trimmed and manicured lawn, the slightly uneasy feeling of foreboding came back to him.

Afternoon tea was in full swing over by the summerhouse, and Charlotte was as jumpy as a caged bird on its perch as she tried to cater for what was, even to the unaccustomed eye, an obvious gathering of mismatches. Even Montague, sinking comfortably into his protective military shell of authoritative control and undisguised bullying, appeared to be well on the way to a truly malodourous mood.

George studied him from a safe distance. Externally he'd always appeared impeccably groomed and well turned out. Even though he was much older than Charlotte, he still maintained a relatively youngish appearance, with a full head of hair – albeit a little greying at the temples – and a preference for the Victorianesque mutton-chop sideburns and moustache. He was, given the recent economic crash, to some degree still relatively wealthy, and the Rushington-Hydes family name could just about manage to command an element of power in various circles. When he so chose, he could be exceedingly influential when it came to business, and charming when it came to relationships with the opposite sex. It had been a combination of all of those facets which had enchanted Charlotte in the first place. In her initial naivety, her imagination and romanticism had created an image of Montague as some kind of dashing hero explorer type which was, in reality, probably only ever to be found in the pages of various women's fiction journals.

By contrast, Charlotte's tolerant and almost overly forgiving nature, coupled with her then youthful inexperience, meant she'd been initially drawn to Monty like a moth to a candle.

Her father, in one of his rare fits of consistency, had taken an instant dislike to the man, to the point where he'd openly and quite vociferously advised against the marriage. Sadly his protests had not been strong enough at the time to pierce through Charlotte's idealism, and come the finish he'd become resigned to the marriage, on the grounds that it would clearly make his daughter a happy woman. Once the marriage was complete he'd simply returned to his much loved enigmatic lifestyle of fads and outré fashions.

The resultant wedding had been reported favourably in the more influential of the society publications, while the honeymoon along the Mediterranean coast also helped maintain Charlotte's childhood infatuation with the romantic side of classical history. Though, as she'd later confided to George on her return, the artworks and sculptures were often far more explicit in reality – especially the high level of sculpted detail – than the images she'd found in the books contained in Dashambly's extensive antiquarian library.

But with his previously failed marriage ending in divorce and his short, but nonetheless successful, military career behind him, Major Rushington-Hydes had been already far too set in his ways for the new Mrs. Rushington-Hydes to have much hope of changing him for the better. No matter how much she tried or, indeed, wanted to, Monty simply continued to bluster and bully, often in an unsubtle manner until, like the rest of those he'd gathered around him, Charlotte had been worn down into a resigned passivity. Anything, in fact, for an easy life.

Not so George, though. Both he and Montague had been conducting running skirmishes for some time. Be it world affairs, politics, social connections, philosophy of life – whatever the subject of discussion it was always a point of dissention between the two of them. George was pretty sure Montague also relished the heated arguments as well. Perhaps even perceiving the confrontational undercurrents as if he were the dominant male, successfully fending off the challenge of some young buck. For George, though, they had always been merely a way of actively debating a topic.

Sometimes though, as happened the last time Monty failed to successfully force his opinion, he could end up becoming almost obsessively childish and tantrumantic towards George.

"And if there should ever come a time, when this country of ours finds itself at war with yet another continental upstart, then it will be to the likes of myself to whom it will turn to – rather than the likes of whelps, milksops and pacifists – in order to secure and assure a victory. For that is exactly what your generation has become, Effinger, mostly ineffectual whelps!"

"Whelps, Major? What a wonderfully archaic expression! I seem to remember Charles Dickens used to use it in his early novels."

The eruption that followed was positively volcanic, but as

George had already moved off to spend time with other houseguests, the Major declared it a victory on the grounds that George could no longer defend his untenable position.

This time, however, Effinger decided he would be taking no prisoners should the chance arise.

And anyway, if what Charlotte had told him was true, then Monty was already more than preoccupied with Michael's exploits. George was pretty sure the Major would be mentally distracted, preparing himself to fight any needed rearguard action against potential embarrassment in front of the Cranfields.

The drawing room and the games room, along with a side entrance to the long disused trophy room, all opened out onto the wide terrace and down onto the immaculately kept south facing lawns – and with the day coming pleasantly to a close – the view of the concrete stand surrounding the summerhouse was impressive.

Charlotte had chivvied the Hall staff to unpack some of the garden furniture from its storage in the loft above the stables, and as George approached he could see various people seated themselves around a well spread table, while other weekend guests made use of several brightly coloured canvas deck chairs and a reclining sun chair set out around the periphery of the group.

The main table was supported in its role by three folding side tables, conveniently placed here and there as required – all of which seemed to push Charlotte's over-attentive hostessing skills to the limit. As she sat down again she saw George heading towards them and immediately started to fluster.

"George! Good of you to join us!" She frantically searched around her for clean china, shaking slightly as she hurriedly put cup to saucer. Then a hand came across and steadied hers.

"Here, let me do that. Give you a chance to rest for a minute and enjoy the afternoon a little." Donna Fairchild's tone seemed to sooth her almost immediately, and with a smile she sat back to let the woman pour George a cup of tea. "Anyway," she continued, still maintaining eye contact with Charlotte, "I'm sure George isn't fussed as to who pours it."

George smiled politely. "Not fussed at all."

Off to one side, in one of several orange and yellow canvas Director's chairs, sat a slim young man with oiled hair, thin lips and sporting a dark black pencil moustache. Trimmed and cut in the Italian style, as was fashionable with London's young socialites, it looked curiously at odds with his pale complexion.

"There's a spare seat over beside me, George. You can sit down here as there's a couple of legal matters I'd like to discuss with you, while you've got the time. You never know, there might be a bit of a bung in it for you as well, if you play your cards right."

Deliberately ignoring Reggie for the moment, Effinger walked over to the sun lounger on which Patricia Cranfield reclined and relaxed, while brother Jonathan had taken one of the canvas deck chairs beside her.

Jonathan Cranfield appeared to be in the throws of rapidly becoming middle aged. With a high forehead due to an early receding hairline, his general appearance was that of a man who, for whatever reasons, was already starting to let himself run to seed – though Effinger conceded he could well be mistaken. He was wearing grey flannel trousers, a white cotton shirt, open at the neck, and the contrast between the material and his skin helped accentuate what appeared to be a slightly yellowish hew to his complexion. It was almost as if he were recovering from a bout of jaundice or some other liver complaint, though he seemed quite energetic and convivial – quickly standing to shake George's hand in greeting.

"Good to meet you. I'm Jonathan Cranfield, and this is Patricia." He swayed a little, seemingly giddy from the sudden exertion, and rapidly sat back down again, panting and slightly out of breath. "Please forgive me – seem to have been like this since we came back from Egypt. Patricia's physician says I've probably managed to contract something while we were out there looking at the digs a month or so ago." He laughed weakly. "Thankfully he doesn't seem to think I've been cursed by one of those pharaohs."

Beside him, Patricia Cranfield looked up at Effinger through the dark lenses of a pair of tortoiseshell sunglasses. She was obviously in her mid-twenties to early thirties, her chestnut hair impeccably Marcel'd, with a petite nose and carmine red cupid-bow lips, from which she removed a cigarette before introducing herself.

"Forgive me for not getting up. We only got back to Southampton two days ago, and what with the travel, and all the packing and unpacking, I fear it's taken it out of me."

Reggie, still vying for George's attention, crashed into the conversation. "Actually I should be the one resting up. Patricia beat me resoundingly after breakfast this morning. I never knew Badminton could be so competitive! The score was four games to one come the finish."

The cupid-bow arranged itself into an exaggerated pout. "Only because you were gallant enough to let me win, Reginald!" To George she added, "He's such a gentleman."

Still looking down at Patricia Cranfield, George said: "He's certainly something, that's for sure."

"I certainly hope so." Patricia said, putting the cigarette to her lips, she inhaled some smoke, then exhaled it provocatively towards Reggie.

In a grumbling voice behind George, Montague said, "You see what happens when you give women the Vote? Next thing you know, they'll be paying cricket, and it will be the men providing the beer and sandwiches." George didn't bother to correct him in regard to the first England Women's Test tour of Australia that had been quite successful back in 1934 and 1935.

Unperturbed Patricia raised herself up on an elbow. "Now Monty, you know we live in liberated times. But I doubt I could successfully defend myself if you were to come bowling at me!"

Puffing his chest up pigeon-like, Montague replied, "Nonsense! I'm sure you'll be more than skilful! We could practice a little later, if you're up for it?"

Charlotte, pushing non-existent strands of hair away from her ear, suddenly spoke up. "Monty? Have you forgotten? We have Michael and Miss Montoya arriving shortly?"

The change in his attitude, from warm and flirtatious to cold and intimidating, was instantaneous.

"To be perfectly frank with you, my dear, whether they

arrive for the weekend, or not, is something well beneath my interest. May I remind you that it was at your behest an invitation was sent? Therefore I suggest it is up to you to both greet and entertain them whenever they deign to arrive."

Charlotte sounded a little pleading. "Monty, you know I have things to arrange and see to before dinner, and it's only polite that one of us should be ready to receive Miss Montoya. Otherwise what will she think of us?"

Staring at her directly, in a calculating and menacing tone, he replied, "I thought I had made it well known to one and all that I have not even the faintest of desires in meeting this," he paused for a fraction of a second, "this young woman which my son seems insistent on foisting upon us. If such has not been apparent already, then I sincerely hope you will assimilate the information now."

Across the summerhouse gathering there was a very uncomfortable silence spanning five seconds before Charlotte hurriedly stood up, cheeks flushed and sniffing several times in her attempts to hold back emotional tears. Beside her, Donna rose, as did Reggie and Jonathan Cranfield, but Montague remained firmly seated. From her sun lounger, Patricia Cranfield's sultry voice broke the silence:

"If it's all the same to you, Monty, I'd like to meet Miss Montoya myself. Gossip aside, she sounds wonderfully continental!"

Unappeased, Major Rushington-Hydes harrumphed, reached into his jacket pocket and withdrew a slim silver humidor. Pulling the cap off, he shook out a five inch long black cheroot and proceeded to wreath himself in a cloud of its aromatic smoke. Moments later, with the impasse unbroken, Charlotte sat down, remaining silent and staring fixedly at the tall hedge running the full perimeter of the lawn.

As George put his cup and saucer down on the table, Donna Fairchild casually walked up alongside him. In a low voice, she said, "I'm a little confused. I understand Michael is bringing Miss Montoya. But why all the brouhaha over her visit?"

"She's apparently Michael's latest intended," George replied quietly. "An exotic dancer, from somewhere Mediterranean, or so I'm led to believe."

"And the idiot is bringing her here for the weekend? Good God, what does he think will happen? I suppose the old goat's going to take it out on Charlotte as usual." The latter was more of a soft spoken thought rather than intended for conversation, but George could tell by the way Donna's jaw was set that there was more than a touch of anger at the prospect. Luckily it was Patricia who unknowingly seemed to defuse the embarrassing situation.

"Oh, Monty, do you really want to throw balls at me? I'm afraid I'm still a little exhausted from the last round of fun and games with Reggie. Perhaps there's another distraction you could recommend? How about you give me a guided tour of your hot house? Didn't you say you've been cultivating orchids?"

Placated somewhat by her interest, Montague's tone was warm and buttery again. "I shall be honoured and delighted to show you some of my finest. In fact, I can honestly say I have several species of Dendrobium ceraula which will blush when they see such a bloom as yourself!" He laughed around the end of the cheroot, hurriedly rose and in almost double-quick time proceeded to march Patricia off around the corner of the Hall, towards the more private walled gardens, and the imposing cast iron and glass greenhouse.

Beside him, George heard Donna mutter, "God save us from old men uttering painful clichés."

As if in reply, Charlotte got up, put her napkin on the table, and then proceeded to head purposefully back up the steps and into the drawing room, no doubt, thought George, to start preparing for the next bout of awkwardness to arrive.

Looking across, he saw Reggie watching his stepmother's progress back into the house. Turning a little absently to George, he said, "Remind me to talk to you later," then to Jonathan he said, "Are you up for a couple of frames of snooker before dinner? Just a friendly game or two. Though if you do fancy a touch of excitement we could always throw in a small wager?"

Giving him little or no chance to protest, Reggie shepherded the slightly confused Jonathan Cranfield back up the steps and through the games room French windows, leaving George alone with Donna Fairchild.

After several minutes of contemplative silence, George said, "You do realise you're an awful fool to keep coming here, don't you."

Donna pursed her lips. "Maybe."

"And by the way, the more you keep supporting her whenever Monty starts to bark and bite at Charlotte, the more it makes it worse."

She smiled. "Really? I hadn't noticed."

"How very Greta Garbo of you."

She laughed. "And that sounds very chorus line."

It was George's turn to laugh. "Believe me, there's more theatrics to be had in any courtroom than even I thought possible." He tried to bring the conversation back on track again. "How's the writing going? I saw some of your novels in several London bookshops. The dustjackets were –" He was about to say lurid, but changed his mind. "Were colourful, to say the least."

"Colourful? Cheap and sensational, as befits the dime novel genre. But they pay the bills and give me time to write quality work under my own name."

"And America? Charlotte says you're getting involved with films and Hollywood."

"America seems quite taken with me at the moment. The trouble is, with all this success, it means nothing unless you have someone to share it with."

"So much wisdom, and yet so little common sense. You must realise that it's total insanity to keep visiting, let alone staying here for the occasional weekend? All it can ever do is make you want to take Montague out around the back of the greenhouses and batter him senseless with whatever blunt instrument comes readily to hand."

Donna grimaced. "Okay, I'll admit my anger rises every time I think of Charlotte being treated the way she is. But it's only natural when you consider what that man puts her through." She looked down as she poked at the grass with the toe of her shoe. "The trouble is, that man is her husband."

"Exactly! Which is why you being here complicates things no end. And not in a good way either."

A little defensively, Donna said, "But Charlotte invites me."

"And that," replied George, in an exasperated tone, "Is the root of the bloody problem! For both your sakes, you need to make your intentions and feelings known to her. At the moment you're just a convenient call-upon. A comforter, if you will." Donna opened her mouth to protest, but George continued on. "Look, I've already been telling her it's in her best interest to leave Montague. Only she's terrified of the divorce procedure. But it's either that, or…."

"Or?"

"Or you and she are making assumptions at cross purposes."

"What?" Donna flushed slightly in embarrassment. "Well, er… I'm not sure why all the concern, but I'm thankful for it all the same."

"You've got to stop turning up every time she dashes off a telegram. It's the only way to make her realise she has to make a firm and life-changing decision. Either she stays with Montague, and accepts all that such entails. Or she buys a one way ticket to New York, and makes a new life for herself in America."

Donna considered the implications. "I see. Well, thanks for the advice – though I'm going to have to think on it some more, before I decide whether or not to take it." She picked up her cup from the table, took a sip of now lukewarm tea, put the cup back on its saucer, then casually changed the subject somewhat.

"I don't suppose you've ever seen The Mesmerising Miss

Montoya's act, have you?"

George, accepting the change of topic, shook his head. "No, I don't usually frequent that kind of club. Have you?"

Donna nodded her head a couple of times. "I think I may have seen posters while I was staying in Paris, five or six years ago. Some Bohemian friends of mine invited me to join them for an evening at the Club La Belle Fantastique, as they thought it would help make for an exhilarating evening." She lapsed into silence until she realised George was still looking at her expectantly. "Oh, sorry, I know absolutely nothing about the woman. But if it is one and the same person, then I know she'll certainly be more than just out of place in this company. At least, from what I saw of her performance in Paris."

From behind them came a slightly distant cry of "Hello!" which prompted the pair to turn to see who was approaching. She was a tall, slim, tomboy-ish looking young woman, dressed in a green and russet tweed hacking jacket, a plaid cotton shirt, generously cut tweed trousers, and what George knew to be well-travelled hiking boots.

With a resounding cry of, "George! I'm parched! Be a sport and pour us a cup, would you!" Fiona Collingwood made her usual commanding entrance.

<h2 style="text-align:center">4</h2>

The little Austrian man came out of his house, hurried down the path and pushed through the front gate, the large sledgehammer resting easily on his shoulder. Turning right, he took a few steps, then mechanically raised the hammer high above his head before bringing it violently down – four, five, six times. Turning round, he retraced his steps back into the house, firmly closing the door behind him.

Effinger looked up at the automaton clock as the brass bell stopped ringing, and wondered who might have bought the piece back from their European travels. Despite its tourist orientated tastelessness, it did manage to keep better time, and sounded less wheezing than the ancient and inaccurate grandfather clock, out in the entrance hall. Whenever that chimed, it always preceded the striking with a sound similar to some mechanical French guillotine being hauled up, set, then dropped. Or so George imagined.

Donna had eventually replaced Reggie as Jonathan Cranfield's competition on the snooker table, and despite his initial bemusement, Cranfield soon found himself two frames down to Donna's excellent eye and rapid cueing action. Dejected, Reggie appeared decidedly irate as he sat down in the drawing room to smoke and flick through a motoring magazine.

George, meanwhile, crossed over to the large console radiogram, turned it on, waited for it to warm up, then set about finding a station worth listening to – or at the very least, innocuous and unobtrusive – before dinner. Deciding on what sounded like a programme of light classical music, he settled down in a nearby chair and closed his eyes. The way things were going, dinner was guaranteed to be very much a fraught, and probably indigestion-inducing affair, not helped by Fiona's late arrival either.

As if on cue he heard her voice say, "Penny for them – unless you're asleep that is?"

Opening one eye, he saw Fiona Collingwood standing in

front of him, scrubbed up and re-feminised, dressed in one of Charlotte's spare evening attires. Despite her height, the rest of her was in correct proportion to her size, which helped to dispel some of her gawkiness. Charlotte, forever the ever ready, always maintained a spare wardrobe of emergency-wear, and after a touch of make-up and a dab of perfume, Fiona could become quite pleasing to even the most discerning of eyes.

The trouble was, she would too often revert to the tomboy side of her nature, which had a habit of unsettling friends and relatives alike. Suitors rarely appeared on the scene due to her reputation for having a strong competitive streak. No man liked to be emasculated, no matter how metaphorical such a process might actually be.

Smiling broadly, she sat down next to him and looked out towards the lawn. The tea things had been gathered up and brought in shortly after Fiona's arrival, and on their return, Patricia and Monty had retired to a pair of sun loungers. They had been placed facing away from the terrace steps, so they looked out over the fields opposite, and had a good view of the sunset. The occasional burst of laughter would often surface from Montague, though the reasons why always remained inaudible murmurs from Patricia.

Fiona's voice broke over the sound of the Bavarian Radio Orchestra's performance of Shostakovich's Jazz Concerto.

"Normally I wouldn't say anything, but their conversation was more than a little fruity the last time I caught some. Makes me wonder why on earth they carry on like that around Charlotte. Or even why they carry on like that at all."

George nodded in agreement. "Charlotte assured me it

keeps old Monty in good spirits which, judging by the promise of a fractious evening performance to come, might all be for the best. Mind you, it still doesn't stop me from thinking that the whole arrangement is more than a little off."

Fiona smiled. "Positively French, don't you think?"

"To the point of being farcical almost."

Reginald tossed the magazine aside and picked up the morning newspaper from the nearby occasional table. From across the room, Fiona asked, "And how much did you manage to lose this afternoon, Reg?"

"None of your business." He flicked the paper aggressively and went back to reading. After a moment he folded it carefully and put it to one side. "Well, if you must know, a little over five guineas. That's why I'm hoping father keeps sweet until after we've had a chat."

George sat up a little. "So how much are you looking to pan from him this time?"

He feigned petulance. "That's rather unkind; but true. I daren't ask him for the full amount, but I have to admit four hundred would certainly help ease the situation a little." Looking over at the pair of them, he added, "I don't suppose either of you would be willing?" He let the question hang for a second, then, "No, didn't think so somehow. Oh well, it's not as if I haven't been here before."

"And that's the problem I have with you, Reggie," said Effinger, coolly. "You keep living at the races rather than living within your means. Ever thought of getting some kind of job?"

"Thought about it, yes; but just couldn't see the fun in it

though."

Fiona, deftly changed the subject. "You don't happen to know anything about this Montoya woman, do you? From what I've been led to believe she's the sort of entertainer who performs in the kind of clubs you usually frequent."

"Hopefully I can live down to your expectations when I say yes, I'm pretty sure I've seen her perform in the past. As I recall, she came on stage wearing less than a well-plucked pheasant – though what there was of her costume was worn in a very artistic and expressive fashion. However, I'm pretty sure that, regardless of what she's wearing when she comes a-calling this evening, father will not be in the least bit amused."

Fiona wrinkled her nose a little. "I'm also pretty sure you'll find some way of turning all this animosity to your own advantage."

"Love you too, darling – and yes, I'd consider it a wonderful stroke of luck should Michael become persona non grata in favour of my own sweet self. But then, that would mean dearest papa would have more of a hold on me than even I might care for. At least this way I can be seen as just a little wearisome; easily fobbed off with another cheque."

Charlotte suddenly dashed in, stood in the middle of the drawing room catching her breath, and to no one in particular called out, "They're arriving!" before turning quickly around and heading back towards the entrance hall, calling out "Jessop!" in an attempt to alert one of the senior staff.

From the sun loungers came another outburst of laughter, but no obvious movement until Charlotte reappeared and almost ran over to the French windows.

In a loud stage whisper she implored, "Monty, please come and be introduced."

He looked up, glared at his wife, but proceeded to half roll half twist hiself up off the sun lounger. Once on his feet, he started up the steps towards the drawing room – stating loudly, "Damnit, woman! I am not some dog on a leash!" Behind Charlotte, Michael Rushington-Hydes entered the drawing room, following in the wake of Rosita Consuela Montoya, and everyone seemed to stop for a moment. Even Donna Fairchild and Jonathan Cranfield had abandoned their game of snooker, and stepped out onto the terrace to watch the proceedings, which gave Miss Montoya as much of an audience as she was likely to get for the moment.

Watching as she crossed the room, George could easily see why Michael had fallen for her. He guessed she was around 5 feet 9 or 10, and underneath the colourful make-up, her skin was coloured a soft golden brown. From the look of her dark Latino eyes there was more than just a hint of Spanish fire, and a smouldering sensuality to her full-lipped mouth.

With her long black hair pulled back, and wearing a sharply cut plain grey flannel jacket and skirt, the low cut peasant style blouse was all the more striking, and revealing. More so to the short tempered Major Rushington-Hydes, now stopped in his tracks half way up the steps, due to his physically lower eye line as Miss Montoya walked out onto the flagstone terrace to greet him.

"I am Rosita Consuela Montoya, of the Sao Paulo Sagestigga Montoyas, and you, I am expecting, are the elder Mister Rushington-Hydes, yes?" She held out her hand towards the Major, a movement which made her bend slightly forward at the waist, casually exposing yet more of her cleavage for the Major's inspection.

Barely able to contain himself, though bound by the constraints of his own masculine code of honour, Montague carefully unclenched his jaw. "Believe me, madam, the pleasure is undoubtedly all yours." Eyeing her still extended hand as if it were a venomous snake, he reached out, shook it three times perfunctorily, then released it.

Miss Montoya shook her head as if to clear it a little. "Forgive me, I am...." She searched for a word, then continued, "Pre-occupied with the troubles of the waterworks which Michael needs to fix for me as soon as he can."

Montague looked incredulously at her. "What on earth are you–"

Michael, seeing his father about to explode, jumped feet first into the conversation. "It's the other car, father. Her chauffeur and her personal maid. The rubber hose from the water pump started to leak, and we only just made it here." He wilted under the furnace-like stare of the old man, gracefully allowing his stepmother to come to his rescue.

"Jessop tells me there's a very reliable garage over at Cresslee. Miss Montoya's personal staff are ready to unpack the luggage, then Michael can drive back in his Packard to pick up the parts needed to repair it. Apparently, even though he calls himself the Automobile Doctor, Mr. Tomlinson doesn't do house calls."

Miss Montoya added, "It is an inconvenience I have to live with. Everywhere here seems uncivilised when it comes to suppliers and parts."

In a brave attempt to defuse the situation, Donna Fairchild hurriedly moved to Miss Montoya's side. "If I may make a suggestion?" She carried on without waiting for the Major's approval. "I can escort Miss Montoya and her staff to their rooms while Michael heads back to the garage." Taking Miss Montoya's elbow deftly in her hand she turned both of them around, and guided her back through the French windows and into the drawing room once more, before the Major's code of honour finally collapsed under the strain of restraint.

As Michael and Charlotte followed them back into the house, Patricia Cranfield said quietly, "Isn't she just wonderfully outrageous? I really must see if I can talk to her, once she's settled for the weekend."

Resisting the urge to clamp his jaws shut once more, the Major replied, "She isn't wonderfully outrageous, as you put it. She is nothing more than some painted Jezebel, a – a strumpet of dubious virtue, and no doubt morals to match!"

Patricia Cranfield put her hand theatrically to her throat. "Honestly, Monty, if you think that of her, what must you think of me?"

Major Rushington-Hydes merely hurrumphed, "She's not in your class, my dear." Still vexed, he decided to have one last walk around the walled gardens. It was something he usually did in order to calm down, and it gave him a chance to catch the evening scented blooms before dinner.

Moving off, he called back to the still bemused Patricia Cranfield, "Your company, my dear, will help to put the flowers in their place."

Reginald watched as Patricia trotted after his father,

muttering almost under his breath, "The third Mrs. Rushington-Hydes? I think not." Then he started as he realised Jonathan Cranfield was still standing close by, staring intently at the retreating form of the grumbling Montague.

Extract from Turncoat
Jon A. Connor

It never rains,

But it pours….

1

Tuesday Lunchtime

From across the hotel room he kept getting glimpses of the Glock G34, snug in the shoulder rig worn by one of the three Colombians. Even the well-tailored jacket couldn't successfully hide the bulge. Every time the guy shifted his weight slightly Eddie Caradine caught sight of the worn, matt black pistol grip out of the corner of his eye. It didn't help that the smell from his aftershave was mingling with that of his own sweat and jamming uncomfortably in his nose. Across from Eddie and his partner, Tony, sat the immaculately dressed character who'd introduced himself as Mr. Jose Martinez.

Jose? Renaldo? Fernandez? It was probably all a load of bollocks. But something was making him tense. Even cool, calm Tony was on edge. They'd worked this routine a dozen times in the past, without so much as a twitch. But something was well off this time. He felt his throat tighten and start to dry up. Something wasn't right, and it had to do with the two thugs Martinez had brought with him. They stood in the far corners of the room like statues – emotionally detached and radiating an air of cold professionalism. Protection was standard in this kind of business venture, and if you didn't protect yourself then you were already dead. It was obvious that Martinez wanted to come across as being impressive. But it was also up to Eddie and Tony to appear as unimpressed as possible.

No, he couldn't put his finger on it, but there was something about the way Martinez had been fucking around with them which made Eddie's head hurt like the onset of a migraine. That, and the fact Martinez never seemed to stop smiling all the time, which was really starting to piss Eddie off.

Martinez cleared his throat, then replied to Eddie's earlier question. "Don't worry. The goods are close to hand. More importantly, for me, you have the money?"

Eddie's turn to smile. "It's nearby."

Martinez tilted his head a little expectantly.

Trying to maintain his smile, Eddie continued, "Naturally we're going to need proof of quality before we're prepared to hand over such a large sum of money."

"You consider six hundred thousand to be a large sum?" Again with the bloody ingratiating smile. Eddie felt his anger start building again. Martinez was rapidly becoming the man with the punchable head. He paused for a moment, forcing himself to relax. Get too tense and everything they'd worked for could blow up in their faces.

"Six hundred? Big money? Not really. I just consider it

good insurance not to carry cash on me, at any time. You never know when someone's likely to try and take it off you, do you? Still, as we agreed, we've brought a hundred thousand in cash – all used notes. The rest will be transferred to your accounts once we're happy."

Martinez spread his hands in acknowledgement. "I can appreciate your cautious attitude and, likewise, I hope, you can appreciate mine." Again with the shit-eating smile, despite Eddie's unsubtle jab.

The air in the room was becoming stifling and Eddie wished one of the hired help would either turn the air conditioning up, or at least crack open a window. It might be freezing and pissing with rain outside, but he could feel his shirt, where it was starting to stick to his back – something else he found bloody annoying, along with the suit he'd decided to wear. Tony also looked flushed and uncomfortable. It wasn't easy for him to just sit there and play support. But if they were going to pull it off then he was going to have to hold it together for a lot longer.

Suddenly Martinez said something in Spanish, or so it sounded to Eddie, and the thug he'd mentally named Mexican Pete moved in from the side. Eddie tensed as the bloke opened the wardrobe, then handed Martinez a Samsonite briefcase. Martinez laid it almost reverently on the low table, thumbed around with the combinations, then popped the catches – the noise of them snapping open sounded loud to Eddie. Martinez lifted the lid, then turned the case around so Eddie and Tony could see the contents. Inside was a neatly wrapped clear plastic bag containing a white, granular powder.

Tony sat back on the sofa and looked at Martinez, eyes

narrowing a little.

"I'm no rocket scientist, but that doesn't look like five kilos of pure to me, no matter how fucking high grade the quality." He turned to Eddie. "I've had enough of this. Let's piss off and Carlos here can keep the bloody stuff. I'm sure we can find some other bastard, nearer to home, prepared to sell us some quality gear without all this bullshit."

Eddie hurriedly put his hand out, stopping Tony from getting up. Somehow things had veered completely off the script, and Tony seemed about to lose his bottle and blow it completely – even before they'd had a chance to get out of the hotel room. He didn't honestly expect the guy to turn up to the meeting with five bags of high grade gear in one case? He nervously licked his lips with the tip of his tongue. The stress was starting to leave a metallic taste in his mouth, which was always a bad sign.

In an effort to defuse the tension, he said, "Chill out a little. Jose is only being as cautious as we are, aren't you." He looked over to Martinez, and saw a simmering anger had crept into the smiley routine.

"If you do not want to do business, gentlemen, then say so now. I am a very busy man," he checked his Rolex, "And I have a flight to catch back to Cartagena."

Snap decision time. Eddie tried to smile. "The cash is only a five minute walk. I take it the rest of the coke is just as close? So, what I suggest we do is this. You, the two of us, along with Speedy Gonzalez over there," he pointed in the direction of the bodyguard who had a thin moustache, "We can step out for a little fresh air. You can show us yours, we'll show you ours, and that way you'll know we're on the up and still want to do business."

The two bodyguards looked across at Eddie suspiciously. The one now christened Speedy Gonzalez uttered a staccato "Que?"

Martinez started speaking rapidly in Spanish again. When he finished he looked over to Tony, his slippery timeshare salesman smile back in place. "When you're ready, gentlemen, we shall adjourn to the car park."

Eddie closed his eyes for a moment, grateful things were getting back on track, and silently hoping Tony would play along with the change to the script. They'd worked as a team for so long, Tony should know he could trust him implicitly by now.

Two heartbeats later he heard Tony saying, "Okay, but if I get frozen you can all fucking stand by." He stood up, wiped his mouth with the back of his hand, then declared to no one in particular, "All this rain is making me want to take a piss every five minutes." Without waiting, he hurriedly disappeared into the bathroom, closing the door hard behind him.

Eddie had felt his gut spasm as he tried to work out what the hell Tony was playing at, leaving him alone with the mark. They'd never split up before – not ever. They'd always worked on trust in the past, always instinctively covering each other's backs, regardless of how the deals went down. He looked sheepishly across to Martinez, and rubbed at his stomach. "I think the pizza lunch was a bit too rich." He grimaced, forcing a belch out for added effect. If this was Tony's idea of payback for him not bringing the money up to the room, then there was going to be one hell of a score to settle when this was all over, that was for sure. Only amateurs and the clinically insane would turn up with a holdall full of cash and not expect to get ripped off the first chance they got.

Martinez's smile disappeared and Eddie knew the two thugs were also getting edgy.

Come on Tony, what the fuck are you playing at?

Martinez made a show of looking at his watch again. "Your partner seems to be taking –" There was a flushing sound followed by the bathroom door jerking open and Tony, adjusting his suit, walked towards the hotel suite door. Pausing with it half open, he looked over his shoulder. "What the fuck's everyone waiting for?" Then leaving the door wide he started down the corridor, heading for the lifts.

*****

As soon as they were outside the cold February wind came at them, bringing with it stinging flecks of ice. Eddie laughed to himself. If you asked any Mancunian bastard if it rained all the time in Manchester, they'd tell you to piss off. But there'd been times since he'd moved up North when he'd wondered what the sun actually looked like. Today was just heavy dark grey clouds and a nagging cold wind. Rounding the side of the building, they stepped off the pathway and onto the exposed tarmac of the hotel car park. Eddie guessed there must have been at least two dozen high end business cars parked around the perimeter. Towards the centre were clumped various people carriers, rag tops, and the occasional 4 x 4. Most of them were crowded up near the entrance, so drivers and passengers didn't have too far to walk before they were back in the warm protection of civilization again.

With Martinez leading the way, the four of them headed towards an impressive Lexus. At least it wasn't a bloody BMW. Almost every scrote of a dealer Eddie knew was driving a BMW of some sort these days. Either that or an Audi. Until they managed to get higher up the food chain and switched over to a fully equipped Merc. Or one of those new, lush Jags. Now, that really would be sweet.

Martinez pulled out a set of keys and depressed the fob, automatically opening the boot. Inside was spotless and empty except for a dull silver flight case, the sort professional photographers kept their equipment in. Another slim silver key and some more dickering with the combinations, then Martinez lifted the lid and stood to one side, letting Eddie and Tony see that the case was full of oblong plastic bags identical to the one still up in the hotel suite.

Snapping the case shut, Martinez said, "Now you have seen mine gentlemen, I would most certainly like to see yours." Eddie only just managed to suppress a snort of laughter, but a glance over to Tony stopped it in time. Tony looked like he was going to shit himself. This one really seemed to be getting to him. When it was all over the two of them would have to sit down and have a talk, because it was becoming obvious Tony had lost his nerve.

In a slightly hoarse voice Eddie said, "Ours is the blue Subaru over there. I'll get the cash then we can go back up to the hotel room. Bring the gear with you and we'll check the weight while you sort out the transfer details." All that honour amongst thieves was just bullshit for the movies.

A short walk, then Eddie popped the boot of the Subaru, grabbed hold of a large canvas overnight bag and unzipped it.

He pulled open the top so Martinez could see the banded stacks of used twenties and fifties, before pulling the bag out and slamming the boot shut. Without waiting for the others he started walking back to the hotel, knowing they would follow close behind.

Later, when he looked back on it with the aid of twenty-twenty hindsight, he felt he should've seen the three thugs earlier. But with the weather and the poor light, he didn't see them until they'd already started to make their move.

The first was a white guy in a navy blue Crombie. His hair in dreadlocks, tied up in long rounded loops – something which Eddie thought looked stupid on most white people. As Eddie's group moved between two rows of parking bays, the white guy was coming in from their right, cradling an ugly looking snub nosed Uzi across his chest, military style.

The black guy with the close cropped skinhead was coming in from their left. He was carrying a massive automatic pistol down by his side – a Walther P99, with its distinctive two-tone colouring – waving it away from his body so not to get it tangled up with his coat. In a strange way it sort of matched the long, olive green Army jacket the guy was wearing, and for some reason Eddie focussed on the small Israeli flag embroidered up near the shoulder. You could pick the jackets up cheap from most Army & Navy Surplus stores. A fully functioning Walther was a lot more difficult to find.

But it was the tall bloke heading directly towards them who became the focus of Eddie's attention. Wearing a long serge overcoat and what looked like a fucking cravat. He was tall, stocky, with a determined expression and a cold smile. Plus he was carrying a sawn off shotgun with both hands, held at hip height, pointed directly at the on-coming group.

Eddie had already started to slow down, but to help emphasise the point, the guy with the shotgun shouted, "You! With the bag! Stay right where you are, fuckwits! Keep on moving and you're fucking dead! That goes for you three pricks behind him as well, especially you with the fucking Charlie!"

Eddie stopped, closed his eyes, dropped the holdall down by his feet and swore under his breath. "Oh Jesus fucking Christ! This day just can't get any fucking worse?" As if talking to himself, he tilted his head up towards the sky, and to no one in particular, he shouted, "If you don't make a move now someone's going to get fucking hurt!"

At that point everything happened at once.

The guy with the shotgun looked slightly confused, but he continued moving forward, feeling himself safe with his two pals covering from the left and the right. Then, seemingly from nowhere, around the car park perimeter appeared a surge of Armed Response personnel. From one of the vehicles nearby came the sound of an over-amplified loudhailer: "Armed Police! Put your weapons on the ground and step away from them now!"

Shotgun looked directly at Eddie. "What the fuck is going on here?!" Only he never got to find out. From the hotel came the sudden explosive sound of Mexican Pete's Glock, followed moments later by a very surprised look on Shotgun's face. In slow motion he fell forward onto his knees, reflexively taking his left hand off the sawn-off to steady himself. But his right index finger, firmly hooked around the twin triggers, clenched in a spasm.

Flame and pellets exploded from one of the chopped down barrels, ripping into the black guy's thigh, knee and shin, effectively taking his legs out from under him. Another spasm sent pellets from the remaining cartridge bouncing point blank onto the tarmac, ricocheting back up like a psychotic swarm of tiny bees and setting off half a dozen car alarms.

Through the roar of his damaged hearing, Eddie could faintly hear some of the chaos swarming up around him. The bullet that'd killed Shotgun, had come from their hotel room up on the seventh floor. As he looked up, he could see the bodyguard's arm, trapped awkwardly between the window and its frame, unable to open the window fully due to the joys of Health & Safety.

The guy had still held onto the Glock even after five or six spider webs appeared on the toughened glass as rounds from the Armed Response rifles punched into the man's contorted body. He was dead before the backup team had climbed the stairs and kicked the door in.

Carefully raising his hands in the air Eddie slowly turned around, looking back at the others.

The black guy was rolling around on the wet tarmac, clutching his wounded legs and screaming his head off. Eddie thought he could see patches of exposed kneecap and shin bone in amongst the tattered remains of his black jeans.

On the other side, Dreadlocks had dumped the Uzi. It was probably under one of the nearby cars. Scene of Crime would no doubt find it when they started their preliminary sweeps of the area.

He looked back again at the remaining three still standing.

At the back of the group, Speedy Gonzalez had grabbed Tony from behind, his right arm firmly around his partner's neck. Only Tony didn't seem to be resisting, or moving at all. Then, as Speedy pushed Tony away from him, Eddie watched his partner fall limply to the damp tarmac, the knife clearly visible as the South American dropped it and kicked it away across the car park.

Martinez was still staring wide-eyed, mouth half open, with a dark patch spreading across the front of his trousers where he'd obviously pissed himself. Over the discordant ringing in his ears, Eddie heard Martinez say in a broad West Midlands accent:

"Fuckin'ell! You two are coppers!"

There was little else Eddie could do. The operation was totally fucked up.

Worse, his partner had just been knifed to death in front of him, and the cold realisation of it, combined with stress, tension and shock, made him feel like puking the pizza back up. He closed his eyes to stop himself from crying out in sheer frustration and rage, barely able to hear the instructions the Armed Response Commander was shouting into the loudhailer. Eddie just wanted to walk over to the bastard, snatch the microphone out of his hand, and tell him that they'd just totally fucked his life up.

Trouble was, he was still under cover.

Keeping his hands on the back of his head, he carefully knelt down, then eased himself forward, face down on the car park tarmac. Putting his hands slowly behind his back, the only thing he could do was to wait for the Armed Response

Team to start doing their job.

2

Tuesday Evening

The conference room of the South Manchester Divisional HQ, at Elizabeth Slinger Road, still held the persistent aroma of long nights and longer early mornings. Ghosts of inquiries past – when cigarette smoke stung your eyes and bitter coffee screwed up your guts for days afterwards. Even after a force-wide smoking ban and repeated scrubbings by hordes of minimum wage cleaners, the room still had an odour which crept up your nose and stayed there long after you'd left the building.

Detective Inspector Mike Fennick caught it as he entered the room. The whole scene was depressingly familiar. Fluorescent strip lighting with establishment cream and green paintwork. Grand Designs, eat your heart out.

Those who had already arrived were either sitting down or gathered around the stainless steel coffee urn and obligatory plate of biscuits. Above them, the clock on the wall read almost 6pm.

Less than four hours after the collapse of Operation Gold Dust, and they're already looking to start the witch hunt.

Fennick kept the thought to himself as sat down at the conference table. As he reached across to pick up a bottle of water and a plastic cup, he said quietly to the person beside him, "Great you made it back, I was beginning to feel like Daniel in the lion's den. I take it things didn't change much after the rest of us left?"

Keeping his voice low so as not to attract attention, Detective Sergeant Steve Hansen muttered, "Still three dead, so no change there."

"Sarcasm ill becomes you."

Hansen grinned a little. "Marcus Swannick is out of emergency surgery and in the HDU until tomorrow. Looks like they've been able to save his leg, rather than amputate. I told one of the nurses they should cut it off first chance they get as it'll make him easier to catch the next time."

"I swear you get worse." Fennick poured some water into the clear plastic cup as Hansen continued.

"That's just for starters, here comes the main course. Mr. Jose Martinez is not even Colombian. Turns out he is none other than Paul Duffley, who is part of Renton Penstone's mob." Hansen adopted an atrocious Dick van Dyke cockney accent. "'E's a tasty Sarf Lundun geezah, with a large firm, an' quite a bit of previous as well, guv'ner."

Fennick grimaced. "Gawd bless yous, Mary Poppins." Hurriedly he sat up. "Looks like the debriefing's about to kick off. Try not to be too defensive if they start throwing questions our way."

Detective Chief Superintendent James Raynolds settled himself down at the head of the table. He reminded Fennick of a stereotypical middle-class bank manager, even down to the little salt'n'pepper 'tash and slightly greying sideburns. Raynolds had been head of Operation Gold Dust, and it was plain he wasn't a happy man. Hardly surprising. He was the one who was going to have to handle the media, take the flack, and try to salvage whatever glory could be pulled from a complete and utter pile of shit.

To Raynolds' right, tall and gangly Chief Inspector Leonard Stopes was representing the uniform involvement. Often unkindly called plod work, uniform had been invaluable when the operation had collapsed. They'd secured the perimeter, logged personnel movements in and out of the crime scene area, and kept the press at arm's length. They were also a partial defence against an ever-increasing sea of administrative paperwork when it came to things like house to house.

To Raynolds' left sat Chief Inspector Ramesh Bashani, head of the Armed Response teams, both in the car park and the hotel itself. Fennick nodded politely to him. They'd known each other professionally two years ago when they'd both been working in the south. Unkindly nicknamed The Major, he was one of the few Armed Response Team members who didn't come from any kind of military background. Bashani smiled warmly, then went back to reading the printout in front of him.

Down the table was Sergeant Lynn McKay. A youngish-looking tech expert, and one of the many women succeeding in the previously male-dominated specialism. She'd been the liaison for the Intelligence Unit that had supported Gold Dust. Down from her was DI Jack Telford, a highly experienced incident manager from the Major Crimes Team, who seemed to have a perpetually harassed demeanour, and an ugly taste in ties.

That left Fennick and Hansen, both included because they'd caught wind of the original lead over on their patch. That had led to another collar which, in turn, had then germinated Gold Dust as a full scale drugs operation. Out of professional politeness they'd been invited to the final stage, purely as observers, which was fine as it meant they were out from under their own DCI's feet for a while.

The only person missing from the debrief was Detective Constable Eddie Caradine. After he'd been located by the command team he'd been bundled off in an ambulance to be checked over and have some stray shotgun pellets removed from his face and neck. It should've been a simple A&E procedure, involving nothing more complicated than a pair of tweezers and a trainee nurse. But somewhere along the line Caradine had been dosed up with sedatives, and had to be ferried back to his flat in a taxi, in no fit state to be interviewed until the morning. Without the undercover DC, Fennick wondered how the debrief could be successfully concluded.

Raynolds loudly cleared his throat and what conversation there was around the table died.

"Lady and gentlemen. I don't have to tell you that the media will be all over this very shortly. Shotguns, submachine guns, police marksmen firing into buildings. No doubt some bastard in the hotel recorded it all on their smartphone and is probably in the process of trying to sell it to one of the cable news companies even now."

Nobody laughed. Over the years it had become common practice that any idiot with amateur video footage, regardless of what it did or didn't show, no longer automatically passed it onto the police as potential evidence. There was money to be had from TV news departments, all desperate to be the first to run exclusive pictures or footage.

Raynolds looked around the table before he continued. "As

it is, everything has been delayed by DC Caradine being medically incapacitated. Now, I appreciate the more time spent in delays means more time for fine details to be forgotten. Which is why I want to start things off now, even though we're short of our star player."

Around the table heads bobbed in agreement. Even Fennick found himself nodding with the pack.

"Fine. Well, Gold Dust should've been a simple operation with no complications. They should have exchanged the money for the cocaine, given us the word when it was okay for us to move in, then left the hotel room so Armed Response could disarm the three of them and make the area safe. All with minimal use of firepower."

Again the collective heads nodded in agreement.

"Okay." Raynolds paused for a moment. "Then what the fuck happened to change the script? One minute we're ready to make the deal, the next we're down in the car park. We knew where their car was – we had both it and them on video and CCTV. We also had them in the hotel room with a kilo of high grade cocaine. So what the fuck were Caradine and Cooke playing at?"

Ramesh Bashani jumped in. "I have no idea what they were up to, but the change of plan left me with little time to split my team and get them into an advantageous position. I was lucky to have several qualified marksmen on the ground; otherwise we wouldn't have been able to deal with the bodyguard in the hotel room. Once he started firing into the car park, there was nothing else I could do but deploy active fire in order to protect those in the immediate vicinity. Thankfully the weather kept bystanders to a minimum."

Ramesh had been the only control officer actually out in the car park, so it had been up to him to make a snap decision regarding damage limitation when the shooting had kicked off. The others had been squeezed into a tiny back office which the techies had kitted out, effectively turning it into an Operations Control Room.

It was all Wi-Fi, Bluetooth – pinhead cameras and audio circuitry that could be discretely sewn into the lapels of a jacket. And, of course, it was no longer about the gathering of information, but the quality of it. Then compiling it and passing it on to the legal experts. It was, after all, the Crown Prosecution Service that would finally decide whether or not they had a winnable case when it came time to prosecute. Legal technicalities still held sway over factual evidence, and sometimes even served to undermine it.

Raynolds, McKay, and Telford, along with Fennick and Hansen, plus Jill Gillian the interpreter, had all been shoehorned into the cramped space. Loaded with an impressive array of portable equipment, all part of the modern Police Ops circus, they'd even managed to bring in four large flat screens. Two had displayed static feeds from the hotel suite, focussed around the coffee table area. The other two had been feeds from Caradine and Cooke. When Cooke had used the toilet just before they left, the team had been treated to the sights and sounds of him urinating, then a view of him in the bathroom mirror while he washed his hands. Fennick remembered him looking uncomfortable and very nervous. Yet, even when he'd had the opportunity to say the magic word, he'd just dried his hands and left. Fennick had been sure Raynolds would call the Armed Response team in at that point, but he hadn't. Nor had he when reception from both of them had started to break up in the car park. Raynolds had hesitated, and that had helped fuel the confusion which followed.

But that was just the way Fennick saw it. Both he and Hansen had been transformed from observers to witnesses, destined to be dragged in front of various inquiry boards until their lords and masters were suitably satisfied.

Lynn McKay, her body language already aggressively defensive, spoke up. "If we'd known about the car park then we would have put directional microphones in place beforehand. There's only so much range you can get out of miniature equipment powered by watch batteries."

In a deliberate tone, Raynolds said, "No one is blaming anyone from technical support for the poor reception, because the car park wasn't in any projected scenario. I just wish we'd obtained more from the hotel room."

McKay brindled, her anger overriding respect. "At the initial briefings we specifically said we needed more time to prep the hotel room, rather than just rely on a couple of fixed cameras. We're tech ops, not bloody miracle workers."

Raynolds snapped back, "Alright! You've made your bloody point!" Then immediately regretted it. "Look, I'm sorry. No one is blaming anyone for anything at the moment." He turned and looked beyond her. "Jack, have we got anything on the three hijackers? The one who died looked like he was running things."

Jack Telford consulted his notebook then, in a steady tone, like a school teacher lecturing a class, he started in on what was obviously a carefully prepared report.

"First off, only two of the Colombians were real. The survivor is Alejandro Lucumi, and the other killed by Armed Response was Sebastian Tulio. They came into the UK via Holland, usually worked as a pair, normally as personal security guards. They're on the NAFIS database for various assault charges, but they've never been successfully convicted. Both are ex-military, but as far as we know there's no particular cartel affiliation. The third, Jose Martinez, is a British national by the name of Paul Duffley. Originally from Birmingham, but now usually London based, though with several addresses to his name."

He paused as if letting his students catch up with their note taking, before carrying on. "Duffley is a known associate of London based criminal, Renton Penstone, and despite the name, Penstone is as Essex as the day is long. We're assuming Duffley is working for Penstone, rather than freelancing in regard to this venture. It's a pretty good assumption that Penstone sanctioned the sale. He's been a high end London dealer and supplier for some time now. No recent record, but that's down to a good defence team and others prepared to take the fall for him." Again a short pause, even though no one around the table had written anything down. After an audible intake of breath he continued.

"Which brings us to the three armed hijackers. Marcus Swannick is in the Wythenshawe Hospital HCU, while they do their best to save his leg. He's a local villain, part of Peter Wainwright's crew, usually involved with prostitution and Internet pornography sites. The other is cooling off in one of the traps downstairs. He's Dillon Nichols, another of

Wainwright's crew, though mostly petty stuff with a bit of dealing on the side. He's waiting for legal representation before we can proceed further. Forensics should have little trouble in connecting him to an Uzi, which Scene of Crime found under a nearby car. As far as they can tell, it's not been used for a while. The barrel has undisturbed rust, and three rounds at the bottom of the magazine were starting to corrode together. Not so Swannick's 9mm. That had been recently cleaned and oiled – a well looked after piece. The rounds in the clip also seem pretty new. They're checking to see if either matches anything we might have open at the moment, but that's going to take ballistics another day or so, at least."

He paused again, this time more for effect.

"Now to the second fatality. The man in charge of the hijacking was none other Edward Victor Carlton."

Hansen tensed at the mention of the name, a reaction not missed by Raynolds.

"Would you care to add anything, sergeant?"

But Telford wasn't going to be upstaged by any interloper. "Edward Victor Carlton – also known as Tiewrap Teddy Carlton – was a long time enforcer, loan shark and general right hand man for Wilson Merrillies. Not quite a local hard case, Carlton worked more around the Ellesmere Port area. The nickname Tiewrap is due to his alleged use of large industrial cable ties. Placed around an immobile victim's neck and slowly tightened until they…." His voice tailed off to an embarrassed silence as he finally realised his mistake.

Face flushed slightly, Raynolds looked thunderously at Telford. "I'm sorry for interrupting you, Jack." He maintained the angry eye contact as he continued, "However, do you still have anything to add to that, sergeant?"

"No, sir. I was just going to say that I knew Carlton of old. He's never usually favoured firearms in the past, but then he's never been in charge of anything in the past either. Everything else is on file. It's fairly comprehensive since his supposed retirement."

Seemingly placated, Raynolds jotted something down in his notebook, then looked back up to Telford again. "Jack. I need you to keep me up to speed at all times. Anything new – literally anything – and I want to know about it. I've a full press briefing at nine-thirty tonight. Hopefully that should keep them busy long enough for them to miss the ten o'clock evening news. With any luck." There was another short pause while he organised his thoughts, then, "Okay. If no one has anything else to put into the pot?" He quickly looked around the table, noting the slight shake of peoples' heads. "No? Okay, I'd like to say thank you to Chief Stopes and Sergeant McKay for attending. If we need anything further then we'll contact you. Chief Bashani, I want you as deputy co-ordinator on this. You'll report directly to me. Jack, I want to see the forensics reports as and when they're in, plus the post mortem on DC Cooke as soon as that's ready. Push for it if needs be. I want to build up a good knowledge base as fast as possible, so we can get this whole thing cleaned up and squared away with the minimum of delay. Inspector Fennick, Sergeant Hansen, remain behind, I want a word with the two of you. Next progress meeting will be eight tomorrow morning. Again, thank you all for your time."

On his way out, Ramesh Bashani patted Fennick on the

shoulder. "Catch up with you later Mike." Then without waiting for a reply he left the conference room with the others. As Fennick refilled his plastic cup, he noticed Hansen had started to tap his fingertips on the table top – getting twitchy for one of his smokes. Fennick had stopped ten years ago, though he always had sympathy for those who were still addicted.

Raynolds continued to write several more lines in his notebook, nodded to himself, then looked up.

"I've not discussed this with DCI Sugden, but I want to bring the two of you in to help with the investigation."

Fennick took a sip of water, and wondered if there wasn't a whiff of internal politics in the air. "Saying our DCI agrees, why should you want us to get involved, sir?"

"This investigation is bound to generate a lot of external interest, it always does when things go wrong. There's media speculation already – they cornered a couple of uniformed PCs before we managed to put out an official press release. I want the two of you involved so as to give us the benefit of an outsiders' view."

A little truculently Hansen said, "And if we find something you're not happy with, then what, sir?"

For a second Fennick thought Raynolds would explode, but he managed to keep himself in check. "Regardless of what you find, you'll report it to me and I'll deal with it accordingly. Whether I like it or not is immaterial. An officer has been killed in the line of duty and I want to know exactly why it happened on my watch."

Fennick tried to placate things. "I think what Sergeant

Hansen meant was how much do we tell the public, if we're asked, and how much is going to be kept under wraps?"

Raynolds looked down at his open notebook. "I'll be the one handling the public and the press calls, so you don't have to worry about that." He let out another long, calming breath. "First thing tomorrow morning I want the pair of you to interview Caradine. I want to know why the change of plan and why neither of them saw fit to call us in when things started getting out of hand. But above all I want to know who the hell he's been talking to. It's obvious someone tipped these people off, and I want to know who."

Fennick was quicker than Hansen. "You suspect Caradine of being the leak?"

"At the moment everyone's a bloody suspect. Even you two."

Fennick kicked Hansen sharply under the table, cutting him off before he could reply. The last thing they needed at this stage was to start antagonising the DCS. Changing the subject, he asked, "You'll clear everything with DCI Sugden?"

"Don't worry about him. Just go and talk to Caradine in the morning. Or, if needs be, bring him back here, I don't care. All I want is his account of the fiasco, and I want it in by midday tomorrow. There's an incident room being set up. It's on the fifth floor. Once you've talked to Caradine, you can get yourself settled in there."

Raynolds slipped the notebook into his jacket, checked he'd left nothing else, then got up to leave. "I'll expect something by tomorrow lunchtime." Then he was out the door, heading back to his office.

Fennick looked down at Hansen's fingers resting on the polished table top. It looked like they were auditioning for a part in a finger-puppet version of Riverdance. Pushing his chair away from the table, he stood up. "Come on, Steve. Let's get you hooked up to a smoke before you kill something."

3

Outside, the back of the station was cold, wet and deserted. Patrol cars were mixed in with brightly marked police vans, while over the other side the on-coming shift were parked up under the harsh yellow sodium yard lights. To the left of the exit door was a large bike shed with a few cycles chained up in it. The command had still to give the die-hard smokers a dedicated shelter, so they had unofficially commandeered it. It wasn't much, but it offered some protection from the relentless drizzle.

Hansen ducked under the roof and took out a flat tin of small cigars. He thumbed a disposable plastic lighter into life and, after a couple of puffs, took a steady draw of smoke down into his lungs. Closing his eyes he felt his body relax.

Behind him, he heard Fennick mutter in a sing-song voice, "We are the Nicoteenies…"

Opening one eye Hansen glared at him defiantly before looking down, watching the glowing coal of his cigar struggle to survive the weather.

"Well, here's a pretty how-de-do, and no mistake."

Fennick dug in his pockets and located his smartphone. "Aye and here comes the rub." He tapped at the screen until he'd located DCI Sugden's entry, looked at the various numbers, then checked his watch. Chances were Sugden had already left the office by now, and he had never been known to divert his office landline. Apparently that was doing humble dispatchers out of a job.

Fennick tapped the home number, heard it ring, then DCI Sugden's voice growled in his ear.

"If this is a dirty phone call, it had better be inventive." Without waiting for Fennick to reply, he continued, "I was wondering when you'd call. From what I've seen on the evening news it looks like you were ragged, bagged and royally shagged from the word go."

"That's one way of putting it, sir. However, it looks like DS Hansen and I are not going to be allowed to walk away from the wreckage. DCS Raynolds wants us to stay on as part of the investigation. So much so he's already assigned us for tomorrow."

"Has he now? That's nice of him. Hasn't said a bloody word to me though."

"Well, we've only just gotten out of a post op wash-up meeting."

"Wash-up? Tell me more, Michael."

He always hated it when Sugden called him Michael. It was always in the same tone of voice like his father used to use when investigating a suspected 'mischief.'

"There was just the seven of us. CI Stopes, CI Bashani from Armed Response, Jack Telford from the Major Crimes Team, a sergeant McKay from Urban Intel, plus Steve and myself. It was nothing much more than initial job allocation and task assignment. CI Bashani is deputy co-ordinator under

Raynolds, and Telford's in as Incident Room Manager. Steve and I apparently provide the investigation with an outside viewpoint. Everything is still through DCS Raynolds."

"Everything?" From the receiver Fennick could hear the muffled sounds of Sugden's television and the distinctive signoff music as the local news slot concluded. Then Sugden's voice again. "Make sure the pair of you keep hold of your notes, just in case. Make copies if you have to."

"Why? Is something up?"

"For a start you've got one dead copper as a result of all this, never mind the villains shooting each other. Plus Armed Response opened fire in a public place. You can bet your last condom the human rights, and other 'concerned groups', aren't going to let a chance like that fade away. Not without using it to generate some kind of self-publicity. Police brutality and Big Brother – though I bet half the buggers couldn't spell Nineteen-Eighty-Four, even if you gave them a head start."

Before he could stop himself, Fennick asked, "How did you know about Cooke being killed? It's not been released to the media yet, as far as I know."

He could picture Sugden, feet up, sprawled across his worn out sofa, grinning like the Cheshire Cat.

"Mancunians. They're worse than fishwives when it comes to gossip, unlike proper Cheshire coppers. Right?"

Fennick groaned to himself. Yet more Force politics. "Okay, sir, understood."

"Right, remind me what the pair of you still have open at the moment? There's the B-and-Es over in Northwitch,"

"Still collating statements. No witnesses, but looking at the MO it's a gang of three chancing it on a regular basis. Trouble is they're getting cockier with every success. Steve still has a couple of outstanding car jackings, plus a domestic with the added attraction of potential ABH. The injured party's going to be in hospital for a while yet, and the woman who put him there is in remand. At least this time the bloke's coming forward and admitting he got the shit kicked out of him by a woman. Not forgetting I'm likely to be invited to the IPCC as part of the Complaints Commission investigation. Hopefully we should have this fiasco wrapped up in a couple of days, but there's obviously no guarantee of that."

"Aye. Well, keep me in the picture as and when you turn something up. Oh, and one more thing. Make sure you put your expenses through on their budget, not mine. Don't want the pair of you thinking you're MPs and claiming twice, now do we. Talk to you tomorrow." With that the line went dead.

Silently shaking his head, Fennick dropped the phone into his pocket. At least Sugden would be happy it was all happening on someone else's patch. Turning his back to the wind, he asked, "How do you know Vic Carlton?"

Hansen dropped the remains of the cigar on the floor and rubbed it out with his foot.

"I knew of him, and in the past I've had to interview some of his handiwork. It's one thing half strangling someone with a length of hard plastic until they agree to pay the interest, or the protection, or whatever. But afterwards it takes a sharp knife to cut someone free, and there's not many places you can cut without seriously hurting the victim. Cut your own throat, or choke to death. Not much of a choice." Hansen shoved his hands in his pockets and hunched his shoulders against the weather. "He should have been put away long ago, but we could never build a solid case against him. And with his reputation, backed up by Winston Merrillies, no one was ever going to come forward and testify against the bastard."

"So before my time then?"

"Sort of. He hasn't been active for about four, maybe five years now. Sold his books to several thugs he'd been grooming for the part. There had been a rumour of a falling out between Merrillies and Carlton, but nothing anyone could officially pin down."

A gust of wind whipped along the open shed. It brought with it heavier rain, which drummed loudly on the corrugated roof. A quick glance at his watch, then Fennick said, "Sod this. Let's see if the desk sergeant can find us somewhere to stay."

Back in the warmth they headed to the front desk and finally located their target. She was a slim, amicable, woman who had kept a touch of grey in her hair rather than dying it out.

"I wouldn't hold out much hope. It's mid-week, so most of the station house will be booked out until Friday."

Fennick smiled optimistically at her. "What about something in the local area?"

"This close to the airport? Look, if the station house can't place you then I'll ring around and see what else might be available. There's a list of approved hotels somewhere around here." From under the front desk she picked up an A4 ring binder. "Here we go. As soon as I find something I'll send one of the PCs to find you. Where are you likely to be for the next hour or so?"

Hansen jumped into the conversation. "Probably the canteen." Turning to Fennick, he added, "It'll be easier to locate us there, rather than the incident room, seeing as that's still being set up at the moment."

"Fine. I can't promise anything mind, but at least it'll be warm and dry."

*****

Once through the double doors Hansen headed towards the servery while Fennick made himself comfortable at one of the deserted tables. The canteen wasn't much above the basics. Pastel coloured utility furniture, strip lighting and a selection of posters screwed onto emulsion washed walls. Still, it was better than some he'd been in when he'd worked down south. A minute or two later Hansen returned carrying two teas. Placing them on the melamine table, he sat down and pulled a Kit Kat out of a pocket. Opening the wrapper he snapped the biscuit in half and offered the other half to Fennick.

"Thanks." Fennick took a sip of his tea and wrinkled his nose a little. At best it could be described as warm and wet. Anything other than that was being overly generous.

After a short period of silence, Hansen said, "What are we doing here, sir? I mean, we were only supposed to be here for the day. Get to see a result, and then back home again. I also get the feeling there's history between the DCS and Eddie Caradine. Hardly surprising, given Caradine and Cooke's reputations."

Fennick looked over the rim of his mug. "I only know some, and most of that's hear-say. It's common knowledge their nicknames were Butch and Sundance. They got results, but most of the other teams considered them a right pair of cowboys. I only met them for a couple of hours, but Caradine gave me the impression of being the wilder of the two." Fennick paused to break off a piece of chocolate. Still chewing, he said, "I know their clean-up rate protected both of them in some circles."

Hansen nodded, indicating the approaching desk sergeant. "Looks like we've at least got an early result on the accommodation."

She looked slightly pensive as she put the booking information down in front of them. "I've found you a couple of rooms at the Grafton Hotel. It's not much, but it's clean and tidy and it won't make too big a hole in your expenses."

Fennick looked down at the address and sighed a little to himself. The Grafton wasn't what he'd call a result at all.

*****

Up in the Gold Dust incident room, CI Bashani watched the last of the IT support team leave, and members of the investigation team start to log into workstations. Grabbing some stationary from a pile of supplies he sat down in front of his own screen, his mind wandering as he tried to psych himself up into making a start. He really was getting too old for this kind of crap. Every year he'd tell himself it was going to be the year he retired. Once his kids finally left for good then he'd take himself and his wife off to the south coast. Or Cornwall. That had always seemed nice. Somewhere with a little bit of sea and some sand. Somewhere that was bloody warm and sunny for a change. He'd only taken the Manchester position because it supposedly offered a better promotion route and pension prospects. Then the recession had started to bite – pay freezes and budget cuts – and it had kicked the tatti out of his savings and group pension funds. One day, though. One day.

Breaking out of his reverie he powered up the workstation, then logged himself into HOLMES2. A few intro screens, then he pulled up a template and started modifying it to suit the initial investigation requirements. Designated statement readers and the office manager would amend it further, but for now he needed something familiar to help him relax before going home. The system was already loaded with information previously indexed when Gold Dust had been sanctioned as an operation. It just needed importing and tidying up. Loading and linking the sections now would help to save time in the morning.

Around him the activity began increasing as others got down to typing up initial reports. Already in were statements from the hotel staff, from the few bystanders who'd been in the car park, and from many of the hotel guests who thought they might've seen something important. At this stage it was impossible to say what information would turn into leads and what might turn out to be dead ends. Everything still had to be typed in handraulically rather than scanned, then added to the database, before the analysts could start. Not forgetting, in accordance with Data Protection procedures and protocols, forms stating that the information had been correctly inputted, would also need to be inputted. And filed. Ad infinitum.

A young DC carefully placed a sheet of paper on his desk. "It's the contact list, sir. The office manager says could you please check through your details and let him know if there are any changes."

A quick flick across the columns – nothing to change. His gaze drifted down the list of names until it stopped at DI M. Fennick. He hadn't seen Mike and Jan in a long time, and there was some catching up to do since their Hertfordshire days. Least of all, how Mike had managed to avoid being charged with assault.

*****

In Raynolds' office the main lights were turned off. Light spilled softly from the uplighters, and from a swan-necked brass reading lamp on the uncluttered mahogany desk. Under the light was the first of Jack Telford's update briefs, giving Raynolds enough immediate material for the 21:30 press briefing, and a list of additional tasks still awaiting completion.

He sat back, rubbing his eyes and pinching the bridge of his nose in an effort to relax before facing the cameras and the press. He still had twenty minutes before he was due down in the Media Room. With his eyes closed, he went back over his mental checklist for the umpteenth time. He ticked off the points he wanted to emphasise, those he wanted to play down, all the while making doubly sure whichever direction the bastards came for him, his arse was well and truly covered. And with one undercover officer killed, along with the two civilian fatalities, he was going to have to keep a very tight control on things. Otherwise they would be like a pack of sheep-worrying dogs tossed a sacrificial lamb.

Breathing deeply, he opened his eyes and reread Telford's brief. Most of it was what Jack had given at the 18:00 meeting, though there was some additional information regarding DC Cooke. The Pathology report stated he'd died almost instantaneously when the tip of the knife pierced his heart. Left-hander Alejandro Lucumi had been carrying the thin stiletto in a custom made sheath sewn into the sleeve of his jacket. It had been a simple case of slipping the weapon free, then sliding the wickedly thin blade into Cooke's back, the slant of the thrust and the razor edges of the blade ensured it would fatally damage vital organs, regardless. He remembered making eye contact with Lucumi as the Colombian was being driven away from the scene. There had been no emotion. No anger, no triumph, no remorse. Just a cold, flat, soulless void – as if he were totally dead behind the eyes.

In fact Lucumi had remained silent ever since his arrest. An interpreter had tried for several hours to get him to admit to his own name, but he'd just sat there; unmoving, uncaring. Raynolds had even brought in a psychologist to check if Lucumi had managed to put himself in a trance by self-hypnosis. Wasn't that supposed to be a conditioned defence against professional interrogation these days? There were dozens of questions he wanted to ask – and not just in regard to the killing of DC Cooke – which he felt sure Lucumi had the answers to.

Paul Duffley, on the other hand, had been quite the reverse. He hadn't stopped talking since he'd been brought in and processed. The trouble was it was all shite. Demands for specific up-market solicitors, phone calls to inform dependents and family, along with wild claims of police brutality if he caught someone giving him so much as a dirty look. Raynolds had told the cell sergeant to shut him down for a while. Let the tosser fester for a bit. Once he realised he was just pissing people off, then he'd be more amicable when it came to interviewing the bugger. They already had enough on him to put him away for a decent stretch, regardless of how lenient the judge might be. But if they could use him to get intelligence on other activities, all the better. Mice to catch rats. Maybe. The problem was, once one had managed to become King Rat, it took quite a lot to actually pull the bastard down.

Raynolds shuffled some of the paperwork around until he came to a photocopy of the file on Duffley. A quick leaf through showed a blank MG6E sheet. So far nothing had turned up which could damage the prosecution's case. But it was still early days. There was also the matter of getting Caradine's initial statement down and on record, so the IPCC wouldn't kick up a fuss. At least having him medically off limits for twelve hours gave the team breathing space to get organised. It also helped to keep him out of harm's way, and the media spotlight, come to that.

He sighed and pushed the papers away from him, then picked up the silver framed photograph he kept to one side of the reading lamp. It was a studio shot of himself, his wife Patricia, and their son, Nathan, when he was a few years younger. Now he was about to graduate from university to make a career out of something. Raynolds thought hard for a moment, but couldn't recall the last time Nathan had mentioned anything about career aspirations. For the umpteenth time he told himself he needed to talk to his son. There again, the way he'd been feeling about life and work of late – not strictly apathetic, more just a general world-weariness – maybe it was time to jack it all in and retire? But he knew he couldn't afford to, at least not in the present financial climate.

He put the photograph back then looked at his watch. Time to greet the lions. He went over to the coat stand, slipped into his uniform jacket and checked himself in the full length mirror on the back of the office door. Since he'd become a desk man he'd dispensed with the clip-on and had taken to wearing proper ties. It was mostly out of snobbery. That, and the fact they photographed better in publicity and presentation shots. He fastened his jacket, and looked himself over in the mirror one last time. No doubt the psychologists would say the uniform was his protection against the pains and inadequacies of the real world. A pseudo-protective shell, from which his ego could happily dictate to his underlings with impunity. And you didn't need a university education to recognise bullshit when you smelt it.

He closed his eyes, building himself up once more, but as he opened the door and stepped out into the corridor, the desk phone started ringing. With an angry grunt of dismissal he waited until the eighth ring, at which point his voicemail kicked in, then closed the door behind him. Whoever it was, he would pick the message up later.

4

Wednesday Morning

In the muzzy glow from the street lighting outside the bathroom window, Eddie Caradine leaned his body, zombie-like, over the toilet bowl. One arm outstretched so as to support himself against the wall, it took him about thirty seconds to finally realise he hadn't freed himself. Having pissed in his own boxer shorts, he was standing near naked and barefoot in a cooling puddle of his own urine – his boxers clinging wetly to his thighs and groin. Through the fug in his head he regretted doing the vodka on top of the hospital sedatives. His tongue felt dry and numb, and his head felt as if someone had their hands against his temples, trying to squeeze his brains out like a teenage zit.

A blind scrabble through the contents of the bathroom cabinet had turned up a strip of old Co-Codamol tablets. He remembered getting the prescription strength painkillers from a little scrote of a dealer, after the last time he'd tried to patch things up with Simone. Everything had gone horribly wrong. Come the finish, she'd ended up slapping him hard across the face. He had reacted instinctively and punched her – thankfully pulling it at the last second so she'd only ended up with a badly bruised nose and 'panda' eyes for a couple of days. He'd gotten the Co-Cos for her to ease the pain for a day or so. But every time he'd rung her old number it'd gone straight to voicemail. Even her few friends had eventually refused to answer his calls.

Despite all the hassle and stress, he was sure he still loved her, and he figured he'd find a way of getting her to take him back. Once all this crap was over he'd see about a transfer to somewhere else – something more conventional which Simone would be willing to accept. She'd never been happy with him doing the dangerous stuff, even though she knew he enjoyed it. He was bloody good at it, too. In fact, despite all the amber flags on his personnel file, he had received several commendations early on in his career. But Simone always wanted him to change departments every time something heavy got splashed up on the evening news. Or at the start of a new assignment, where he needed to be away a lot, doing surveillance and getting himself established. She'd become more insistent about it until finally, after the arguments had become explosive, she'd kicked him out. Or he had left. One of the two. Anyway, doing undercover work wasn't going to be the same any more. Cookie had always been there to cover his back, and he knew he'd never really trust anyone else like that. Not again. Not with his life.

Popping a couple of the plain white tablets into the palm of one hand, he turned the cold tap on and cupped the other into the stream of water, then tossed the painkillers into his mouth. Quickly sucking up water from his cupped palm he hoped he could swallow without triggering any gag reflex. The way he felt at the moment, if the tablets stuck in the back of his throat he would puke his guts up for sure.

He turned the tap off, shut the bathroom cabinet door, then started wondering why he was still standing in a puddle of his own piss. Clumsily he peeled off the wet boxers and peering around the dimly lit bathroom he located a crumpled towel. He'd thrown it back into the bath after the last time he'd actually taken one, which had been Monday afternoon. He picked it up and half-heartedly used it to rub his groin and legs dry before finally dropping it onto the floor in a half-hearted effort to soak up the rest of the urine.

He wandered out of the bathroom and through the bedroom, picking up a discarded pair of jeans and oversized sweatshirt as he went on through into the lounge. Finally dressed, he crossed to the wardrobe style doors which hid the tiny kitchenette. Opening them wide revealed a small sink, a two-ring hotplate, and a microwave. All the modern comforts of home. He grabbed the kettle; half filled it, and stuck it back on its stand. As it started to boil he rinsed out a mug, dropped two teaspoons of coffee and three large spoonfuls of sugar into it, then followed it up with boiling water.

Under the TV, the display on the DVD player showed 04:30 a.m. as he sat down on the sofa, carefully sipping at the hot drink and trying not to burn himself. He was going to need all his wits about him later on, especially when the post-op inquiry started to get going. Perhaps the Co-Cos, the caffeine and the sugar wouldn't be enough. From the low table in front of him he prodded at the collection of remote controls before he picked up one more battered than the rest. Peeling back the sticky tape which held the broken battery cover in place, he lifted the lid and took out a little Ziploc bag of powder.

Just a little lick. To help with the healing process.

*****

Steve Hansen slowly started to climb back to consciousness. Strange beds and unknown surroundings always meant he had a lousy first night's sleep. He'd finally awoke just before half six to find himself lying diagonally across the hotel double bed. Sometime during the night the covers had been pushed to one side, and now the sheets were damp from sweat caused by the heating still full on. Not because he'd been cold, but because he'd been unable to find a way to turn the bloody thing off.

He slowly worked himself free of the top sheet, gathered it up into a large ball and tossed it to one side. He slid off the end of the bed, padded naked across the nylon carpet and threw open the curtains. February was a really depressing month, especially this early in the morning. Outside was still dark and cloudy, though the lights from the traffic moving along the M60 didn't seem all that sparse. Welcome to Manchester: a city that never sleeps. He opened the window as far as he could, letting the chill air cool the room and his body for several minutes before he turned back to look at the dishevelled bed. Bloody depressing or what? Glancing at his watch didn't help any. It was that stupid time of the morning. He could drag out his shower and shave, dawdling around for the extra half hour, or he could remake the bed and try to catch another ten minutes sleep. But he knew, as soon as he tried to settle back down, his mind was going to wander and he was going to end up thinking about Felix again.

*****

Mike Fennick woke slowly; languidly he turned over, stretching under the bedclothes, savouring the last fleeting moments before having to start in on what he knew was going to be a long and probably painful day. It had been late by the time he'd returned home. He'd taken one look at the name of the hotel and had immediately recognised the franchise. He also knew from past experience, how the chain always strived to live down to its well-deserved reputation. Even though he expected their part in the investigation to last only a short time, he'd decided he would rather long-haul the distance from home to the Greater Manchester South station than risk staying at the Grafton. It meant early starts and late returns, but then, what else was new?

Beside him, Jan started to gently snore, her face turned

towards him on her pillow. She had been out at one of her evening group meetings and had probably come in around midnight. Whatever time it'd been, he couldn't remember her getting into bed beside him.

They had been together for nearly ten years, and neither had ever mentioned the M-word during that time. He thought about it for a moment and wondered why they both shied away from becoming what his mother would have called "legal and decent." Maybe there was still an appeal to the debauchery supposedly inherent when the two of you are "living in sin."

But if there was then it was somewhere in the background, buried under all the bills, sacrifices, commitments and responsibilities they both helped to carry in order to keep their relationship working.

Looking at her face he could see where a crease in the pillowcase had gently worked itself a little way into the corner of her slightly open mouth. The result was a wet patch slowly spreading as she continued to dribble in her sleep.

If only his phone wasn't still in the pocket of his trousers.

Careful not to disturb her, he eased out of bed, lifted his dressing gown off the nearby chair and put it on. From the wardrobe he collected underwear, socks, a fresh shirt and a plain tie. Sticking his shoes in his dressing gown pockets, he picked up his suit off the back of the chair. For a moment he reconsidered capturing Jan with the camera in his phone, but then decided his testicles were best kept where nature had originally placed them. Silently he closed the bedroom door and headed into the large, open plan living area.

They had been lucky to get the 'modern style' warehouse loft conversion when they did. True, it had a twelve foot high ceiling, and the mass of historically preserved cast iron supports and crossbeams reminded him of a giant Victorian railway station. But the solid concrete floor required to support the listed metalwork meant they were pretty well insulated from any potentially noisy neighbours below.

From the basket by one of the large windows came a slightly startled "Mr'owl?"

Belladonna, Jan's large pitch-black cat, rudely awoken by his movements. They glared at each other for several long seconds before the cat's head slowly disappeared back down into the basket again. If ever there was a way of measuring evil, then on a scale of one to five, the cat was sure to register a six.

Mike smiled as he went into the guest bedroom and turned on the shower in the en-suite bathroom. All things considered, life could be a damn sight worse.

******

Hansen was already standing at the Grafton Hotel's entrance by the time Fennick drove up. The weather was still foul, though given the choice Hansen found it more preferable than waiting in the reception area. Fennick's car was warm and still smelled of air freshener. Comfortable, with the radio tuned to Piccadilly, but turned down low and in the background. As he clicked his seatbelt home, Hansen dispensed with the usual morning pleasantries.

"So what's first on the agenda, Boss?"

Out of the corner of his eye he could see Fennick frown a little. He wasn't the Senior Investigating Officer on this one, and it was common knowledge he always disliked being called Boss, but Hansen felt a little payback was in order for being abandoned in favour of the joys of home comforts.

"If we see any place that looks good for a breakfast then we'll stop. If not, it'll be straight to Caradine's flat. According to the hospital, he should be fit enough to give a statement."

Hansen nodded, then let the radio fill his attention for a while. They were already losing time by collecting information from Caradine at his home. Why hadn't he been interviewed directly at the scene? His injuries were, according to the ambulance staff, uglier than life threatening. He could've been taken back into the hotel before going to the hospital, or taken straight to the booking station and the on-call doctor. The wounds were messy and uncomfortable – ugly where some of the pellets had lodged under the skin – but it was nothing to stick him in an ICU for. Having him booked and processed under his assumed name would've at least meant he could keep his cover intact and probably uncompromised.

Fennick glanced over at Hansen. "What's up?"

"Sorry?"

"You're too quiet, so what's up?"

Hansen shifted a little in the passenger seat. "Nothing… Something… I don't know. Could we just go and take Caradine's statement? The sooner we do, the quicker we can get back to our own patch."

Keeping his eyes on the congesting motorway, Fennick smiled. "You're not telling me you're missing Molly already, are you?" Molly was DCI Roger Sugden's unofficial nickname when out of sight and earshot. Around several of the Cheshire stationhouses it was rumoured if you spoke his true name three times while looking in a mirror then, like the Devil, he would appear behind you.

"No, it's not that, it's just…" Hansen looked out the window at the cars travelling alongside them. "It's just a feeling, nothing more."

"Christ! First Sugden won't tell me anything, and now you go all Mystic Meg on me."

A little aggressively Hansen said, "Look, it's something you said last night about the pair of them being a right couple of cowboys. And I don't like the fact one of ours got killed in the process…" His voice seemed to trail off and he went back to looking at the cars in the adjacent lane again. "I also don't like the fact we thought it was going to be some standard business with a Colombian wholesaler, when clearly it wasn't. Okay, if we can connect something back to Ren Penstone, then fine, but how the hell did that connection get missed in the first place? And that's before we try and sus out how Wainwright, or Merrillies, or who-bloody-ever got wind of it all. And why did Alejandro Lucumi and Sebastian Tulio kick off the way they did? I can understand the shooting – you can put that down to protecting your team. But why kill Tony Cooke?"

"And you figure Caradine and Cooke for some of that?" Fennick sounded concerned.

"That's it – I just don't know. And I don't want to go making Caradine fit if he's had nothing to do with it. Does that make sense?"

Fennick nodded, more to help settle Hansen, rather than

in total agreement. "Okay, we'll go talk to Caradine first, but if there's time then we'll be stopping off for brunch – I can feel my cholesterol level falling already."

They followed the M60, then onto the A57 towards Rusholme and Longsight before taking side roads and backstreets, until turning into the bottom of Carpenter's Road.

Fennick let the car slowly crawl towards the five story block of flats where Eddie Caradine was living. In the half light of morning he could see that more than a few of the cars parked up by the kerb had For Sale signs clearly on display. With cheap SIM cards, it was easy to run a kerbside dealership and not get done for illegal trading. Given the on-going recession, the dodgy traders were coining it in. Finally he found a space close by and parked up. With a touch of luck it wouldn't get keyed before the interview was over.

Caradine was on the top floor, and coupled with the surprise of the lift actually working, there was also a distinct smell of disinfectant in the background. It was good to know people were actually doing something about the quality of their lives, rather than just sitting around blaming the police, the rich, the councils, the government, or whoever they thought was the cause of all their woes were this week. But it took a concerted effort, and some places were happy to shut their front doors and let the low-life get on with it.

At Caradine's flat Hansen pressed the doorbell. From somewhere inside they could hear the muted sound of a buzzer. A pause, then the sound of movement from behind the door as Caradine opened it. He was wearing washed out jeans, local market trainers, and a baggy grey sweatshirt with some kind of American university emblazoned on the front. As he stood looking at the two of them, both Hansen and Fennick registered the slight contraction of his pupils and the vague furtiveness as he looked towards the lifts. The left side of his face was still patched up with several two-inch square pads of cotton dressing, held in place by strips of papery sticky tape. As Fennick looked closer, he could see dark spots where some of the pellet wounds had seeped through before they'd finally stopped bleeding.

Automatically Hansen started to flash his warrant card, but Caradine just turned round and headed back into the flat. "Come on in. It's not as if I haven't been expecting you. Just didn't expect you this early."

The front door led straight into the living room, and walking around the sofa towards the open kitchenette, Caradine said over his shoulder, "Tea? Just about to make one for myself."

Fennick shook his head. "Not for me, thanks. We don't want to keep you too long. Just wanted to see if you felt up to giving us your account of what happened yesterday."

Unperturbed, Caradine looked expectantly over to Hansen, who had already taken a notebook and pen out of his jacket pocket. "No, I'm fine as well. But thanks for the offer."

While Eddie threw a teabag and boiling water into a cup, Fennick and Hansen settled down in the two easy chairs either side of the large sofa.

Sitting in the middle of the sofa, Caradine cleared a space on the coffee table and put his cup down. Deliberately he looked expectantly from one to the other, then back again, and Fennick started the interview.

"DCS Raynolds has decided to keep us on while the Gold Dust investigation gets underway. We're here to get your account of yesterday afternoon, though we both appreciate it's not been the easiest of twenty-four hours. However, the sooner it's processed then the sooner we should be able to close things."

Eddie let out a short, barking, "Ha!" then grabbed a battered packet of cigarettes and a disposable lighter off the coffee table. Without asking or offering, he lit one up, sat back, and exhaled the smoke loudly. Fennick continued unperturbed.

"As I said, we know it's not been easy, but best to get this down now while it's still fresh in your mind." Deliberately he looked over to Hansen. "Sergeant?"

Hansen cleared his throat as the smell of the burning cigarette made him realise he hadn't had one himself since leaving the Grafton. "Can you give us your movements for the last twenty-four hours?" He tried to make it sound as casual as possible, not wanting to create any animosity early in the interview. "Start from the time you left this flat, or went out to meet anyone. Did you stay in Monday night? Or did the two of you go down the pub, or out for a meal? Anything like that?"

Caradine looked suspiciously at Hansen. "Hold on. Am I a suspect or something? Are you making out I had something to do with the whole thing going tits up? Because if that's the case then this stops right now, and we can start again when there's a federation rep here with me."

Hansen sounded a little exasperated, "No one's setting you up, or accusing you of anything." Then, to reassure Caradine, he added, "C'mon Eddie. You know the score, probably better than we do. We've got to be seen to be squeaky clean, and that means eliminating everyone involved in the operation. It's just routine statement gathering. Plod work, for fuck's sake."

Caradine gave another short laugh of contempt, but after a moment's contemplation he launched into a detailed rundown of his movements, starting with the Monday prior to Operation Gold Dust.

Keeping a casual ear on the conversation, Fennick didn't seem to hear anything which sounded even a little off, and as he recounted it, Eddie Caradine sounded confident and unhesitating – the account clear and concise, seemingly free of any obvious inconsistencies. Fennick let his gaze wander around the tiny, one bedroom flat. It had been bigger at one time, but 'Property Developers' had thrown up dividing walls in their efforts to minimise space and maximise their income. So maybe Caradine wasn't the tidiest of people and the flat wasn't in what you might call a comfortable district. But then being undercover often meant you had to rough it in order to maintain your credibility.

He also remembered a seemingly casual conversation about a week ago, in the run-up to the operation itself. When he and Hansen had been invited back to the operation as observers, it had felt like some kind of This is how we do things in the City thing. Typical sort of stunt DCS Raynolds was noted for. Raynolds had also suggested that he and Fennick should "touch base with the guys at the sharp end." So they'd both met up with Eddie Caradine and Tony Cooke on the Saturday evening prior to the final takedown. They'd all gone to a backstreet Chinese which Cooke said was well off their regular patch – far enough to stop them being seen and recognised while they were still working the operation. Fennick had to admit to a touch of admiration when it came to undercover work. It wasn't always successful, and it came with the risk of being exposed, but at least they were actually doing something constructive.

During the evening, Raynolds had come on like some Army Field Marshall who thought the war was already won without even going into battle. His attitude had clearly rankled Caradine, though it'd been Cooke who'd become the more introverted as the night went on. Fennick mentioned it when they were down to coffee and fortune cookies. Tony had brushed it off, saying although he wasn't superstitious he still didn't want to jinx the operation by being too cocky.

But no matter how often Fennick replayed that evening over in his head, he couldn't remember anything which might have indicated something was wrong. They'd both seemed like honest guys about to set up a heavyweight dealer and supplier.

Bringing his mind back to the present, Fennick listened to Hansen reading Caradine's statement.

"So you're saying you stayed over at Cooke's flat the night before last. The pair of you ordered a takeaway pizza and watched a couple of films. After that, an early night, with an early start in the morning so you could be fitted out with surveillance kit."

Caradine kept nodding his agreement. If he didn't agree with it all then he wouldn't sign it, and no signature meant no validation – which meant it could, and probably would, be contested later.

Hansen finished, then looked up and stared hard at Caradine.

"Are you absolutely sure you never talked to anyone about any of this?"

Caradine closed his eyes, deliberately taking a deep breath before replying. "We stayed in, watched two or three crap movies, then Cookie went to bed and I slept on the couch. In the morning we got fitted with fibre optic cameras and mics, then went up to the room at the hotel to wait for the bastards to turn up. I only stayed at Cookie's place because it was nearer to the exchange point."

He snatched his packet of cigarettes up and angrily lit another one, his third in quick succession since Fennick and Hansen had arrived. It didn't help that Hansen's own nicotine threshold was starting to wear thin.

In an attempt cool tempers down and regain Caradine's confidence, Fennick said, "Off the record, what do you think went wrong with the operation?"

Caradine looked down at the filter tip trapped tightly between his two fingers. "I don't know. The Colombians were definitely out to fuck us over, though I don't think they'd tumbled to the fact we were undercover. At least not until the shooting started in the car park."

"So why go down to the cars? I thought the plan was to run the deal from the hotel room?"

"Because we had to make Martinez show us the rest of his gear. The same way he thought he had to make us show him the bag full of money. That's the way it works in these sorts of deals. If we'd gone swanning in there with the cash in a bag we'd've looked like a right pair of fucking amateurs. Straight off they would have suspected something was wrong, and going by what happened outside the hotel it wouldn't surprise me if they hadn't thought about shooting us right there in the bloody room. We said at several briefings we weren't happy bringing a load of loot into the hotel – especially when almost all of it was counterfeit shit pulled in from that raid up in Edinburgh a year or so ago. But we were overruled by shiny-arse Raynolds." Caradine's contempt for the DCS was obvious as he met Fennick's gaze. "So Cookie and I took the initiative and decided to leave it in the car." Calming down again he looked back at the remains of his cigarette. "As it turned out, it really didn't matter one way or the other. We were both set up by somebody else who ambushed us in the car park, so someone's been taking to someone they shouldn't have."

There was a touch of accusation to his voice which rubbed Hansen up the wrong way.

"It certainly wasn't us. We were dragged into this right at the end and, to be bloody honest, we have a whole shit load of better things to do than fuck about in the rain, watching a simple operation turn to utter rat shit."

Fennick immediately stood, breaking the aggressive tension building between Caradine and Hansen.

"Okay, well, I think we've got enough here to take back with us. If you'd just sign the notebook we'll get your account onto the system and that should keep Raynolds happy. For a while, at least." He waited until Caradine scribbled what looked like a signature under the last line.

"Okay, no doubt you've been through similar post-operation routines before, but," Fennick paused for a moment, wondering if Eddie Caradine was actually taking any of it in. He appeared to be distracted, looking intently down at the low table and nudging several of the remotes around with a finger. Doggedly Fennick carried on. "But you're now being placed on post-operation leave. However, you are to ensure you are available for interview at any time until the investigation is closed. No doubt the IPCC will be in touch, and you may want to talk to the Federation and have them assign you a dedicated legal rep for the duration of this investigation."

Caradine still kept his gaze on the coffee table. Fennick nodded to Hansen, and without saying a word, the two of them left Eddie alone with his thoughts.

Extract 2 from Catch a Falling Star
Kelly Lewis

Journal Entry Dated Friday July 11th 1975

Oh, God, am I tired! Friday night, and I can barely summon up enough energy and enthusiasm to write this, let alone hit the high spots. The trouble is, like Shirley Bassey, I've been burning my candle at both ends – and not in a fun way either.

I've been pocketing some overtime cash by doing extra day shifts at the Brunchy Burger Bar. But, if that wasn't enough, I've also been doing some late night film work for an Australian art student friend, Julia D., and her project, Les Morts dans ma Tête ("Which, of course, is your actual French," to quote Kenneth Williams, for The Dead in my Head.)

She's been working on the concept for some time now. It's all allegorical, about how Bettina – the lead – has always felt herself to be misunderstood, boxed in and totally compartmentalised by her life. So when she dies – at the start of the film, naturally – she doesn't realise it and so her mind tries to organise some kind of escape.

Julia says it's all very Cocteau and Fassbinder, though to be honest I can't see it myself. Still, she always gets excited whenever she mentions them, which I suppose gives her a certain element of artistic integrity. Well, if you're going to steal, then why set your sights on just second rate?

As it was, the whole business came about from a misunderstanding we had over a staff-discounted Brunchy Burger Breakfast Special lunch, several months before. I still don't remember much about it because I was still preoccupied with the lion suit I was having to wear in order to promote the new Jungle Burger. It wasn't so much the suit itself, just that I kept wondering half the time if the itching was down to the material, or because Malcolm – the guy who had worn the suit the week before me – had supposedly caught a dose of crabs before he left.

We sit at a table at the back, and after about a minute Peter drops off a couple of still warm Breakfast Specials, along with an untouched bowl of chips courtesy of a departing lunchtime party of eight from one of the local office blocks. Julia then gives me one of her crooked grins from across the table.

"They're doing a fucking brilliant retrospective overnighter at the Scala this weekend," she says in her conspiratorial voice, the volume pitched at around 100 decibels while her Antipodean accent manages to mutilate the word 'Scala' so that I'm saying 'He's a Koala from the Scala!' inside my head for hours afterwards. "D'ya want to come with me, or what?"

To be honest, I'm only really half listening. I'm still in total automatic mode – and desperately trying not to claw at my crotch in public with my free hand – so I just nod my head a couple of times while I psych myself up for the last few hours of my shift, and before I know it I've agreed to go with her. There was this strange sort of mutual pause of surprise from both of us, then she's gushing about it all.

"It'll be bloody bonza, mate! You bring the food and I'll get us in. According to one of the projectionists I was swapping spit with recently, they've found some of the original German and French prints! Isn't that fantastic, or what? And no bloody subtitles either, so there's nothing to distract you from the plot for a change!"

Distract you from the plot? Do they have that basic cinematic essential in Arthouse films?

Anyway I'm that desperate for her to leave me in peace I even agree to meet her outside Kings Cross tube station on the Saturday night for a few drinks and film talk before the screenings start, just after the pubs close at 11pm.

She's got a membership discount card which gets us both in for 25p each for the whole night. The Scala has made its reputation on a daily changing programme of the strange and the totally obscure – and most of the die-hard members probably think Cocteau and Fassbinder are too commercial. Certainly didn't stop a lot of the other serious weirdos turning up though.

By the end of it all we were both hyped up on leftover Hawaiian Luau Burger E-numbers and additives that we're chattering like monkeys as soon as we're out into the sunlight again. At one point I say: "I still don't see what the difference is between those sex scenes and everyday pornography."

She frowns at me, all serious. "For one thing the lighting's miles better and the camera work is more bloody artistic. When Grisobella is laying there on the big mattress getting her brains banged into the middle of next week by the biker?

The close-up shot where the brass bedknob finally falls off and rolls onto the floor is a post-modernist metaphorical statement on the ephemeral nature of the Male in general. Otherwise why call it a knob in the first place? And you don't get that in Debbie Does Dallas, do you?" I give her a quizzical look, and she amends it to: "Okay, well, Billy Does Boston, then – or whatever the equivalent is."

Actually it was Michael Does Man-Hattan – Uncle Tony, who used to work for some Maltese businessmen near Soho – had an 8mm print of it. Left it in his car when he came to visit the family one Saturday afternoon when I was 12. Danny Anderson's dad had been into holiday movies and Danny had 'borrowed' his dad's projector. So we watched it in his dad's shed at the bottom of their back garden – both of us hitting puberty so fast the sonic bangs would have dislodged roof slates.

So, for the second or third time this month I get roped into doing some more acting work for her. She gets us together and says she'd looking to create an air of desolation, so we all end up traipsing out to some deserted industrial estate at two in the morning. We had to help with the equipment, and even the lighting was on batteries so as to keep the silence intact on the soundtrack, rather than having generator noise all over it. "It'll create an air of authenticity," she says, but I know she can't afford the studio re-dub time.

It quickly becomes very much a case of shoot and run – especially towards the end of the scene when we disturb some security dog and end up having to get our arses up and over the bloody perimeter fence. Juliet, however, is totally over the moon about it.

"Ab-so-fucking-lutely great footage! Emotive, energetic,

exciting! We'll have to re-write the script in order to use it, but it's fucking brilliant footage. Hope the lab doesn't screw it all up."

She's shooting everything on old black and white 16mm stock which she picks up for virtually nothing as it's past its sell-by date. Gets it from some odd looking guy who seems to have canisters and canisters of the stuff, and reminds me of some shady little barrow boy. Not that Juliet's worried too much about the quality, mainly as she's also sleeping with a guy from the Kodak processing labs over Harrow way who's developing the batches for sex. Talk about prostituting yourself for your art. She's also getting everything tinted up in sepia-tone rather than monochrome, which gives the editing party screenings a strangely Victorian feel to them. It's all very Independent Arthouse stuff, which is why we're all doing the work for free.

First Person Singular
Dan Meyers

The accommodation at the Old Lodge motel on the edge of Daxton isn't pretty. The only time that would apply is if you put the word 'crap' after it. Still, beggars can't be choosers. Not that I'm a beggar.

The single room is kitted out with a basic bed, chair, desk-cum-table. The wardrobe's one of those cheap flat-pack build-it-yourself – which is probably why the doors don't quite fit together. Tracks worn into the cheap blue carpet go from bed to wardrobe, via the small wash basin. Mirror over the top of it is actually bolted to the wall. Who the hell would want to steal a mirror?

I check the burner phone. Minimal functionality and no GPS. The display shows a quarter after midnight in soft green figures. It's probably still not safe to go out just yet. Too many potential dangers. I put it to one side and go back to watching the neon lights from the strip mall opposite as they flash and dance on the carpet. I pulled the curtains shut several hours ago, but the red and blue lights keep finding ways to insinuate themselves through the chinks and cracks. It's hypnotic despite the wayward spring in the chair continuously poking me in the back. When I first tried to get comfortable it'd been a real piss-you-off aggravation. Now it's something to focus on, keep me awake. Just in case….

I can feel myself mentally sliding again.

*****

Standing in front of me is my father – a Saturday Night drunk who extended it to the other six days of the week as well.

"You hear me, boy?" A big ex-steel plant man, knocked low, to the point where he could no longer get regular work. He'd staggered up from the worn out sofa in front of the TV. I was still standing in the doorway – home late, and I hadn't prepared his supper. When you're 16, with urges, you tend to lose track of time. It'd been happening more and more. He'd then start shouting, coming towards me while unbuckling his belt. "Going to have to strap some sense into you. Something I should've done after your mother ran off."

If I was lucky, before he got to me I'd turn and run out of the house, down the drive and hide under one of the neighbour's parked cars. It'd become a regular thing. As regular as a set piece played out at a college football match. Only the players didn't have scars when they'd not been agile enough. He'd then stand on the porch steps, looking all around for me. After a handful of minutes the near-empty bottle of bourbon would call him back into the house. I'd wait another five or ten, just to be sure he wasn't faking it, then come up from under, and make my way over to Mallory's Diner. Maxine, one of the waitresses, would take pity on me. She'd feed me fries, maybe a burger now and again – or, a piece of pie.

But after a while I'd gotten tired of running. The next time he'd tried it I didn't run. I waited until he was fumbling with his belt, then stepped forward and kneed him a couple of times in the balls – quick and forceful – so it finally registered in his dinosaur brain, and he'd gone down, belt still clutched in his right hand.

While he was wheezing and gasping I got his pants off, yanked down his boxers, and stuck his left hand in his crotch. It took several attempts and a few kicks to his stomach before I'd finally got the photograph right. The little camera might've been plastic and cheap, but it took photographs good enough.

I didn't go back home for several days. Maxine was always happy for me to sleep over, even though she knew I was under age. But when I did go back I still had to be careful.

He was sitting on the sofa, watching TV when I walked in. Didn't even turn round to see who it was.

"So you finally came back. Knew you would." He took a long pull on his beer can, then belched. After he wiped his mouth I started in on my piece.

"I want you to listen to me, and listen good. Things are going to be very different from now on."

He snorted, finished off the beer, and crumpled the can. I waited for him to say something, but he didn't. So I carried on.

"Don't you ever try and take your belt to me again. I took photos of you, and the next time you try anything. and I do mean anything, I'm going to tell everyone that you abused me. That you've been doing it for years."

He snorted again. "No one's ever going to believe you."

My turn to smile. "I don't care if they all believe me or not.

That kind of thing will stick to you like shit on a blanket. Just takes one to start with, and they'll tell some people, who will tell other people, and just like a forest fire, it'll spread all over. Plus I've got the photographs. And the scars as well."

That'd shut him up. Even stopped him drinking for several days. But like a truly unrepentant alcoholic, it wasn't long before he'd crawled back into a state of spiteful remorse.

In the end no one went to his funeral. Not even me.

After that it'd been easy to exploit small town sympathy and gain knowledge of small town indiscretions.

*****

My foot twitches, bangs up against the sports bag, and I'm back watching the lights.

Martin Crowley, the bank manager, will claim $500,000 was taken, even though we both know the take was far less than that.

"It's all insurance, John. People do it every day, inflate their claim, so why should the bank be any different?"

"But won't you get audited?"

"Sure we will, and they'll fine all the money is missing."

I open the bag and look at the mass of money bricks and the loose notes stuffed in around them. First thing to go will be the wrappers, then check for any sequential numbers. They were supposed to be all used notes, but it always pays to be careful. All together it should be a touch over a quarter of a million. I thought it would've been heavier, but it's probably less than 10lb, spread out in a football bag.

I smile at it all. "Go Cubs!" Then feel a little embarrassed, talking to myself and feeling like I was a rookie line-backer again.

*****

The original plan had been Martin's. We'd been sitting in Chequers Bar & Grill on Main Street, around 8pm. I was slowly drinking a beer to pass the time when he walked in, sat down beside me at the bar, and ordered a large Regal and rocks. The drink arrived, and a quiet minute later he'd said:

"We've known each other for some time now, John. Would you say I was a bad man?"

I wasn't too sure as to where the conversation was going. "Not as far as I know, Martin. Why? You looking to confess something?"

"Not as such, but they do say that sometimes a thought is as good as a deed."

"And you've been thinking?"

"I've been thinking. About how to rob my own bank."

"And why should you want to do that? You don't strike me as someone on the breadline, or running short. Unless you've been spending more than you've been earning?"

"No, you're right, Ellie and I are better off than most in town. Kids don't want for anything. The mortgage is discounted through the bank and easy to keep up. Hell, even our relationship is still sweet after the kids left."

"So why the thoughts? And why are you telling me?"

"Well, if I were to put it down to anything, then it would be pure greed. Nothing more, nothing less. As for telling you? Well, I figure, what with your position, you're the best person

I know who could help pull off a robbery."

I looked at him. A now-not-so-slim mid-40s ex-jock, dark blue suit, white shirt and dark tie. Little beads of sweat on his upper lip, caught in the evening stubble.

"How many have you had, Martin?"

"First one of the day – including the cabinet in my office. Still, it's taken some time to grow the stones to talk to you about it."

I'd tried to sound confused rather than curious. "So why should I come in with you on this venture of yours?"

"Same reason as me. I know what you get per month. Less bills and outgoings. But there are all those cash deposits you drop into your account on a regular basis. I suspect they're just donations to the John Cheslin Appreciation Fund, but I doubt it would take much to correlate someone's outgoings with your incomings, now would it."

I'd remained silent, the back of my neck suddenly hot and damp. "Are you trying to blackmail me, Martin?"

"Ah, John. Blackmail is such an ugly word. But I can't think of an alternative right this minute."

"And after?"

"When it's all over we'll be equal in what we know about each other. Knowledge is power, as you obviously know. Sharing it with each other is our safeguard. Think on it."

We'd gone back to drinking in silence, and I'd left shortly after. It wasn't until three weeks later that we'd met up at the bar in Chequers again.

Martin came in, sat down beside me, ordered me a bottle

of imported Crystal Dark and himself a Regal and rocks.

As the barman moved on down to the far end of the bar, Martin asked: "Have you come to a decision regarding my proposition?"

I took a pull from the beer bottle, paused to belch discretely, then said, "I've had a little think on it all. First off we're going to need three extra bodies in on this. Two for the muscle and a wheelman. I need sketches of the inside floor plan, camera locations, details of the surrounding area, number of bank clerks, security guard's details."

"But you know all that, John. Hell, you even know old Frank. He's as local as you and I."

"And that's going to be the problem. I'm not looking to have someone decide that this was an inside job. We need to create the credibility that someone has studied and noted down details. Make the sketches on plain paper, no company watermarks. Maybe even photocopy the photocopies half a dozen times so they start looking fuzzy. That way they'll look good."

"Okay, so tell me the rest of it."

"Simple. I'll be on the inside, distracting Frank. The three walk in, all calm and no panic. Then they go bat-shit crazy, pulling out weapons and telling everyone to get down onto the floor."

"But the bank staff are going to be safe behind bullet proof glass."

"Which is why they'll be shouting to them to open up the side door otherwise they'll start shooting civilians."

"Okay, they've all been told to co-operate wherever

possible. They open the door, then what?"

"Simple. Two of the three get the cashiers to clean out the tills and the reserve safe, then go back out the main entrance."

"And you?"

"I'll be keeping Frank from trying to use that fuck-ugly old Magnum of his while the robbery's taking place. Then I become their hostage, and we'll make good our escape."

Martin had put his empty glass on the bar and waved the bartender over for a refill. He took a sip from the refreshed glass, then half looked at me. "Sounds like you've got it all wrapped up. You got a team in mind?"

I'd smiled. "The less you know, Martin, the easier it'll be."

*****

I'd gone over the State line, then cross county until I found a place with no obvious connection. Then I'd started to use a non-descript hotel – the Belmont – over the following dozen or so weekends, until the manager and I were on chatting terms.

"I wonder if you could help me, Archie."

"I can try, what's the problem."

"I need to pick up a gun."

"Dobson's is pretty fair when it comes to cost. He's the only gun shop around, but he won't gouge you on the price."

"And that's the problem. I'm looking for something that's off the grid."

"And you figure I'd know where to get something like that?"

"People trust you, Archie. You have a thing for knowledge

– and knowledge is a valuable commodity these days." I dug my wallet out and freed up two $20s.

Archie looked at them, fingers reflexively twitching a little in a grasping motion. "And if I did?"

"Then the forty's yours, no strings, provided the information is good."

"Okay," He thought for a moment, then, "There's a place out on the edge of McCarthy creek –"

"Which is an illegal biker bar." I hooked the two notes securely back into my fist. "I might not've been here long, but I do basic research, so I know that's a place I'd have a mind to avoid."

"The only other place I can think of is The Duce, over in Jess'ville. Richard Deveraux will sell you something. Or part trade if you've any Oxycontin?"

I gave him a half smile. "Why, look at you. Drumming up trade for Mr Deveraux. Maybe I should drop by McCarthy creek after all. Tell them you're his agent."

"I'm offering information, nothing more."

"Then let's hope there's no surprises when I meet him."

*****

As it turned out Deveraux was an old-fashioned dishonourable Southern gentleman from somewhere along the bottom half of the Mississippi. His security was called Clyde, who had biceps the size of melons and that twitchy, shiny look of a compulsive steroid abuser.

"To what do I owe the pleasure of your company, Mr Radford?"

The two of them were sitting in the back booth of the bar, away from the overhead lighting and by a window, the top half open to keep the smoke and heat at bay. Clyde stood, silently patted me down, found nothing untoward, but remained standing, blocking anyone else from passing by us.

As I got myself settled I answered his almost rhetorical questions. "Well, sir, I understand that Archie Meritson may well have spoken to you regarding an item I'm interested in acquiring."

"That he has. Did he pass on the cost of such a thing?"

"He mentioned a figure, but I suspect it also included his brokerage fee." I handed him a sealed envelope. "I trust you'll see that he gets it."

Deveraux smiled, showing just a hint of teeth. "You let me worry about that sort of detail Mr Radford. Clyde?" The other man didn't move, but it was obvious he was waiting for the next statement. "If you would kindly give Mr Radford his birthday present."

Clyde went over to the opposite booth, picked up a holdall half hidden under the bench seat, and took out an oilcloth wrapped object. Placing it in front of me, Deveraux flicked the ends of the cloth open, exposing a small black steel .32 automatic and a pocket box of ammunition. There was some wear on the grips, but the barrel looked clear of any rust, and the ammunition seemed relatively new.

Deveraux leaned in and dropped his voice down low. "This came down from New York, and the numbers have been removed so they won't show up in any acid treatment. There's 8 in the clip and 12 still in the box."

I refolded the cloth, pulled a Benny's Big Burgers bag from my pocket, and slipped everything into the takeaway bag.

Still leaning in, Deveraux added, "We would be willing to buy that back from you at a later date, and an obviously reduced price, on the understanding that you don't add any more history to it."

I smiled and got up to leave. "It sounds like a pretty good deal, though I can't guarantee anything, one way or the other."

"Think on it. I'd hate to see a nice piece like that become discarded in the heat of the moment."

Deveraux kept eye contact as Clyde moved to let me leave, though I didn't feel really safe until I was back behind the wheel of an old beater I'd picked up for the duration.

*****

I reach down to the ankle holster, take out the .32 automatic. It looks ineffectual, but I've seen .22 revolvers used in disputes where one side or the other had not walked away from the conflict.

*****

It had taken around another couple of months to start putting the crew together. Martin was in no hurry what with the robbery being motivated out of greed and not necessity.

There had been four of us. Murry Wilson, Floyd Barrett, Barrett's sister Carrie Ann and myself. Carrie Ann had been the driver. Mousey brown hair cut short – Pixie, she called it – brown eyes and a slight dimple in the middle of her chin. "Driver? I think you mean Wheel Person, Aaron. This might be a dead end spur off the 'I', but you still need to move with the politically correct times."

She had a way of laughing that felt natural and unforced, as if she were one of those people who, no matter what, always saw the bright side of things. I'd like to say that she'd felt an attraction to me, but whether it was real or encouraged by her brother didn't matter to me. Friends are friends, but business is business.

She'd also doubled up as one of the masked bandits who stayed close to the bank's main doors. Last one in, first one out when everyone was moving for the exit.

I'd started grooming Murray Wilson first. I'd made him my 'favourite drinking buddy' from a sports bar three blocks away from the Belmont. He was short of money, long on resentment, and perfect for being worked into the role of a liberating bank robber. He recommended Floyd Barrett as his wing man, and Floyd's older sister, Carrie Ann. Floyd had a little record, all petty stuff, which he'd freely admitted to at our first meeting.

Wilson and Barrett had agreed to meet me in The Home Run sports bar, and they appeared beside me as I was part way through a Bud. They took bar stools to my left, ordered a couple of beers and bourbon chasers.

When the barman moved off, Wilson said, "Aaron, this here is Floyd Barrett. Floyd, Mr Radford here has a proposition for us."

Floyd looked at Wilson as if he were some kind of local idiot, then at me. "I hear you have money problems."

I nodded. "You could say that. The bank is about to foreclose on us as we haven't been able to keep up the mortgage payments. By the time they finish adding up the outstanding interest, plus administration fees, then selling it all, it'll leave us with barely enough to keep our heads above water in a rental."

Wilson nodded his head. "We hear you." Then he went back to sucking on his beer bottle. Floyd was more astute. "We?"

"Wife Susan and little Shelby. He'll be 4 come September. The redundancies hit us hard as we were both working for the same company. Dual income to zero almost overnight."

Floyd didn't comment, so I continued with the story. "You can only survive for so long, especially when there's nothing else to go to these days."

Wilson looked over to me. "You not a college boy?"

"Blue collar all my life."

"And you think a bank robbery would solve everything?" His head tilted a little to one side as he asked the question.

"Maybe not everything, but a whole heap of the problems would go away. We'd certainly move. West coast somewhere. I keep reading about old ghost towns out that way that're being reclaimed by people in similar situations."

Barrett said, "And you're prepared to risk it all?"

"I've got nothing left to risk except my family, and I'm keeping them out of all of this."

He nodded. "Wise move. How long you been planning?"

"About a year. I've already got floor plans, camera points, alternative routes in and out of town should we ever need them. I'm not just going at this head on. I need this to be a success."

Barrett took another pull from his beer, tossed his bourbon down in one, then said, "And afterwards?"

"I know someone who'll buy my cut of the money, 75 cents to the dollar. I've been told he's reliable. If you want, I'll ask him if he's interested in taking your cash on as well."

Barrett paused. "Would I know him?"

"Probably not."

Barrett smiled. "Then we'll take our chances with our cut of the money."

I decided then it was time to get agitated. "Well, are you in, or am I just wasting my time?"

"You have the plans on you?" Wilson asked.

"I might be new to this but do I look stupid?"

"Point taken." Barrett took another sip of his beer, then, "Supposing it all comes off, what's the getaway?"

"We take the car down to Ellesmere, switch it there with a pre-parked vehicle, take that cross country to Felton, switch again, then one more at Blixby. From there we head on to the forest just outside of Daxton. I've checked out an area in the woods by one of the old open mining sites. From there the three of you go your way and I go mine. I'd suggest just the one car for the three of you so as not to attract any attention. We use the area to split the takings, and then go our separate ways from there."

Barrett ran the tip of his tongue over his lower lip. "Murry says you're going to be on the inside taking care of the floor security guard?"

"Yeah. I know Frank from way back. I'll be keeping him

distracted when you three come in. Once the money's bagged you grab me as a hostage. That not only gets me away without any suspicion, but should make the local police cautious when it comes to pursuit. Changing cars in quick succession will throw them off vehicle and plate recognition. I make it back into Daxton on foot. I give the authorities descriptions of three random people I've seen while I've been down here, and after they're through and I'm back with my family, the following night we skip, using an RV I've already stashed away."

Wilson said, "See? I told you he had it all planned."

Barrett still didn't seem satisfied. "What's to stop us from just shooting you and making it a 3-way split?"

I took my smartphone out of my pocket. "Apart from the fact I've been stream recording the three of us to cloud storage? Susan has an envelope with the account and password details. It's the same as my living will, so she's not suspicious."

Barrett smiled. "Murry's right. You do seem to have it all planned. And you've no problem with Carrie Ann coming in on this?"

"If she's as good a driver as Murry says she is, then what's to worry about?"

Barrett finished off his beer. "She's ex-Army. Got herself a medal or two for seeing action. You might have seen her around. Drives a red '95 Dodge Avenger."

"As long as she can get 4 low profile vehicles, and remembers where she parked them, then fine."

"No problem. When are you looking to do this?"

I put the gun back in the ankle rig and try to work out how I'd send it back to Deveraux. Putting it back in circulation would be better than just dumping it. He'd sell it on quick enough. I allowed myself a quick smile. That would really piss in the evidence pool. I'd thought about taking a small screwdriver and sliding it several times up and down the inside of the barrel to make some new score lines to help slow down any forensics ID. But they'd show up new if the gun was found too early, and I doubted Deveraux wouldn't waste time holding onto it.

I check again and the burner phone shows 23:51. Getting close to time.

******

On the day everything had gone according to plan. By 11:15 I'd been talking to Frank for a couple of minutes.

"How are the kids and grandkids these days, Frank?" Basic conversation friends tend to make in passing. I'd moved in front of him, blocking his view of the main glass doors, counting the sweaty seconds off until the three of them came running in, waving weapons and shouting through monkey masks like some outtake from a cheap remake of Planet of the Apes.

Frank immediately became hyper edgy, and started to unclip the holster on his belt.

"Better not, Frank. Nothing is worth becoming a dead hero over." He looked somehow crestfallen, until I mention his grandchildren again. All the while the other three were shouting for everyone to get down on the floor and toss out their wallets, bags and mobile phones. As planned, Barrett had gone directly up to the glass shielded counter, Wilson following several paces behind him, while Carrie Ann kicked the wallets and phones into a pile and scooped them into a lightweight canvas sack.

Still with my back to them, I got down on the floor, taking Frank down with me. Barrett, running true to script, shouted:

"Open the side door, and start putting all the money into this bag. No dye packs, no trackers – nothing that will get some of these innocent people out here killed."

The cashiers complied with the company's co-operation briefings because no bank wants the publicity that their actions got any of their customers killed. Barrett stayed the customer side of the door, watching them dump banded blocks of notes and lose money into the sports bag. Back on the main floor, Carrie Ann held up the canvas bag, indicating she's picked up everything worthwhile.

Wilson checked the stopwatch around his neck. "Thirty seconds…. Fifteen…. Five…. And we're done here!"

Barrett grabbed the money loaded bag, pulled the security door shut, then headed for the main doors. As he passed Wilson, he shouted, "Grab a hostage – the one over by the security guard."

Wilson came over and kicked the sole of my shoe. "Hey, you. On your feet. You're coming with us."

I'd paused for a count of five, which was the agreed cue before Wilson said, "Either you come with us, or I shoot you and your fat fucking friend here."

I stood up and let him pull me out through the main door

and around the side of the building where Carrie Ann had parked the car. Barrett and Wilson went in the back and I took the front passenger seat as Carrie Ann drove the car out of the alleyway as fast as she dared, horn blasting so as to clear pedestrians from the entrance.

As we shot down Main Street, Wilson and Barrett had dumped the cell phones out the back windows before we'd gone more than a couple of blocks. Quicker and more efficient than trying to disable GPS, and stolen phones hold little value these days.

Then the monkey masks came off and were stuffed into the canvas sack. We'd planned to burn them in the forest so as to stop any DNA profiling. Leaving them out in the open would've degraded anything, but Wilson was paranoid about such things.

In reply Barrett had just said, "You watch too much CSI on cable." But he'd left it at that.

As we went past the city limit, I turned in my seat and held my arms out to Wilson.

"Okay, tie wrap my wrists."

He'd pulled one out of the bag, then hesitated. "I don't see the point of this part."

"Because it'll give me abrasion marks and bruises, otherwise my kidnapping will seem fake."

I'd made sure he'd pulled the plastic strap tight, then turned forward and started to push and work against them. After I'd started to bleed from the chaffing, I turned round to him again.

"Okay, now cut them off."

Both of them had looked at the cuts around my wrists. Barrett had shook his head. "Shit. You really do take this seriously, don't you?"

"You either buy in one hundred percent, or you get caught."

*****

In Ellesmere we changed to a Nissan, then in Foxton we changed and drove out of town in a non-descript beige Prius, all the while the money safely out of sight in the trunk. Blixby left us with a Chrysler, which was when I'd taken over the driving. It was partly because I knew where we were going, and Carrie Ann didn't, and partly to let all three of them start calming down and come off the adrenaline highs they were on.

By the time we made it up into the woods beyond Daxton, the sun was starting to touch the horizon, casting a glow over the water.

I'd picked the spot carefully. Off trail, and close to the ridge of an old abandoned open cast mine. Over the decades since the 80s and 90s the pits had filled with water. They were deep enough and the water filthy with God knows what so you couldn't see the bottom, even from up on the cliff edge.

Since circling around Daxton city limits I'd been passing a hip flask between the four of us, only I made sure I never actually drank anything from it. When the two in the back held onto it, Carrie Ann had been a little jealous.

"You better save some more of that for me, hear?" They passed it forward, and she'd taken a long pull on it. A minute or so later I took a sharp left onto a dirt road, hearing Carrie-

Ann laughing at the way the two in the back were now sliding around, seemingly a touch drunk.

I passed her the flask again. "Here. We're nearly there so a couple more shouldn't hurt."

True to form, she slipped the neck between her lips and took a couple of swigs. She handed it back to me, saying, "That doesn't taste like common or garden bodega brand."

"Hardly. I figured something like this would call for some 25 year old quality. Let's face it, it's to celebrate our success."

In the back, Barrett and Wilson would've probably nodded their agreement, only the Rohypnol had steadily kicked in, doing what it did best. As I finally pulled into the clearing Carrie Ann seemed to realise something wasn't right, but by then it was too late to worry about such things.

After making sure all three of them were fully incapacitated, I'd gotten out of the car, took the money from the trunk, then went over to a large rucksack I'd hidden a week before. I transferred the money from the large black holdall into a nylon sports bag that had garish orange and neon blue panels and a local high school football team logo on it. Then I'd spent a couple of minutes going through the wallets, clearing out the ready money and anything else that might be useful later on. I still needed them and the canvas sack for the last part of the plan, but it seemed too much of a waste to just junk everything.

Putting on a disposable clear plastic rain poncho and rubber gloves, I went back to the car, gathering up some loose rocks on the way and putting them in the sack with the wallets. I'd dumped that by the driver's door, then went around and dropped the empty robbery bag and the rucksack into the passenger seat foot well alongside Carrie Ann's legs. Wilson and Barrett were still under the influence of the whiskey and date rape cocktail, but it was clear they were fighting it and slowly coming out of its control. I wound down the window, shut the passenger door, then opened the back door. Wilson started to loll to one side as I wound down the door's window, which gave me cause for concern that the drug was wearing off too quickly. Time to move things along.

I bent down, took the .32 from my ankle, then shot Murry in the temple. The poncho caught the blood splatter, and the gloves the GSR, which was why I'd packed both in the first place. I closed the door, went around the back of the car, and did the same to Barrett. His eyes might have twitched as I pointed the gun at his head, but that close up I was guaranteed a kill even if he'd succeeded in moving.

That just left Carrie Ann.

It had been tricky and more problematic moving her from the passenger seat, but after some flipping and flopping around I'd managed to get her securely behind the steering wheel before opening the driver's door window. Once everything seemed to be in position I pulled the automatic from the ankle holster again. I had no idea just how much she'd comprehended when I'd shot Wilson and her brother, but I suspected she'd already figured out what the outcome was going to be, regardless.

Somehow the belief of her knowing it was inevitable made things rest easier on my conscience. She seemed like the kind of woman who might've believed in Fate.

Another temple shot, then I arranged her feet on the

accelerator and brake.

With the dirty work all done, I took off the poncho and gloves, and tossed them in the back with the two bodies. After that, firing the ignition was easy, but keeping some pressure on the brake pedal while I shifted the car into gear was tricky. With one hand on her knee keeping the brake pressure up, I gave the engine around 30 seconds to get warm again, then picked up the canvas sack and dropped it on the accelerator. Moments later I knocked Carrie Ann's foot off the brake and pushed myself backwards out of the car. The engine roared, burning gas as it shot forward, and in less than five seconds it'd became airborne as it sped off the cliff edge. For a moment it seemed suspended even though its momentum kept it moving forward, like one of those cartoon characters who doesn't realise they're treading air until it's way too late.

And like all those characters, it swan dived down, breaking the surface of the lake with a loud splash.

The engine had died immediately. Then the water found the open door and windows, pushing the air out and letting the car sink rapidly to the bottom of the pit. As I looked over the edge, all that was left was the occasional fart of air breaking the surface, and a thin oily residue that was already dissipating as I cleaned up the site.

*****

The strip mall was almost completely closed by 1am, but I gave it a little time to clear. The last thing I needed was for someone to remember me leaving the motel and make my way to the bus station. My feet were a little sore from walking cross country from the camp site back into Daxton, but the short journey was the least of my discomforts when compared to the money in the bag.

At the terminus I put the sports bag into a long stay rental locker, paid cash for a 60 day period, then I asked at the ticket counter if they could break a dollar so I could make a phone call.

"No problem, buddy. The phone's over there. Doesn't get much use, but then I figure that's all down to everyone having cell phones these days. Me? I can live with or without them, it don't bother me either way."

I nodded my thanks as I picked up the four quarters and moved off to the wall mounted pay phone. Lifting the receiver I dialled a well-remembered number.

Ray Caulfield answered on the second ring. "Sheriff's office, Deputy Caulfield speaking."

I could hear the tension in his voice.

"Hi Ray, it's John."

"John! I mean, Sherriff Cheslin, where are you?"

"I'm over the line, in a town called Daxton. They dropped me in the woods before they took off. Can you send a team out to the Old Lodge motel? I'm just going to rest up there until you guys come and collect me. Don't forget to let the local boys know what's going on. I know I wouldn't like it if strangers turned up unannounced, no matter how well their intentions might be. Plus it's their jurisdiction, not ours, so they'll probably want to pick it up from here."

"What? Yeah! Sure! You sit tight John! The rescue party'll be with you as soon as I can get it on the road! Just remember that."

"Good to know, Ray. After the day I've had it'll be nice to

see a friendly face or two."

 # Breakdown on the Galactic Highway

Dave Perry

The man on the bar TV
Says "Wheatballs!"
I look at the alien beside me
It looks back at me
We both know the danger of breakfast cereals
I get us another round of beers
And sip the top off mine
It slips a 'finger' into its glass
And chugs down half in one go
I figure, with the engine bust up the way it is
And spares not due
Until the next meteor shower
We could both do with a rest
From covert blockade running

The man on the bar TV
Says "Fruity Taste!"
The alien next to me
Looks at me with
Two eyes close – but the other three are open
'Strawberry?' it telepaths
I snap my fingers three times
In confirmation, of sorts

But still unsure – last time
It experimented with fruit it was hallucinating for days
The visions became so weird and wild
That even I had to
Disconnect my receiver
To get a good night's sleep

The man on the bar TV
Says "Vitamin Packed!"
The alien looks across
At the entertainment module
It starts playing of its own accord and then
it's 2155 again
Jean and the kids, laughing
And smiling, alive once more
Even though, by 2283
They were all dust
You ride the crest of the light wave and Time
Unravels like threads
From the fabric of Reality
And there's no way in Hell
You'll knit your life back together again

The man on the bar TV
Says "Sunshine Goodness!"
I look at the alien
Remembering the Solar wind burns
It took as it repaired our craft from the outside
How it had sloughed
Two thirds of its mass
Until it had stabilised itself

Finally letting me
Come off the Love-Hate rollercoaster
of emotions
I never knew I felt
Or would ever admit to
In an insane world it's the
Sane who wear the straightjackets

The man on the bar TV
Says "Thermostatic!"
Out of boredom the nanotechbots
Have built themselves an
A.I. module that now wants to teach them all
about morality
My wrist implants tap-tap-tap
Impatiently on the bar top
Wondering how long
It will be before the little
Micro-mechanisms sacrifice the module
on the altar of Science
But only after
They have repaired our craft
Rebuilding their own Universe
They are their own Gods

The man on the bar TV
Says "Crispy Texture!"
Data assimilation complete
The alien beside me
Telepaths "Let us Rock En Roll,
Kimo-sah-bay-bee"

Breakdown on the Galactic Highway

I smile, feeling its
Feathery touch on my face
As I sym-link us
Back together again
We are once more in control of our destiny
Or so we like to think
As we start to surf the next event horizon
We kiss the Light Fantastic
Heading off to our next port of call.

Memindip and the Persian Poet
Jay Andrew Connor

(This is the second in the Memindip series – the first is, at present under consideration by another publisher)

1

As my on-again off-again friend, Adagouti, will readily tell you, Life can become very complex. Especially the second time around, as a Private Investigator.

– Death still has her eyes on you, Memindip. She is like a leopard who hasn't eaten for a week. She's hungry for you.

– But I still have the good favour of Be'kal?

– For the moment. But he won't protect you forever. You need to prove you are still a righter of wrongs, a voice for the innocent, an avenger for justice. You just have to keep doing that in order to keep the Higher Powers appeased.

– But apart from having Tomaso Akriki's body and odd memories, I am still Memindip, of the Lazera tribe, a noble North African off-shoot of the Psylli.

Adagouti glares at me like a lioness defending her kill.

– No. You are the late Memindip, of the long departed Lazera, who was caught trying to cheat a Portuguese trader by selling him quartz instead of diamonds. The fact that he killed you with an ornate dagger in 1701 is a moot, albeit understandable, point. The fact that the wandering remains of your tribe buried you without correct ritual and ceremony, creating your corporeal presence, is not a moot point but the bane of my very existence!

Adagouti has never forgiven me for the mistakes he made during my rebirth. His wrinkled, tortoise-like head bobs up and down several times, then he says:

– As you are now an investigator, you'll need to find a new cause to champion. It's the only choice you have if you wish to keep this second life of yours for as long as you can.

I'm about to ask where I would find such a thing, when the ringing of my alarm clock on the nightstand brings me back from my dream land.

Background noise outside from the city street mixes with that from inside my 4th floor manzil, which means Marzouk is already preparing breakfast.

I wash the sleep from my body then offer up a short prayer to Opoula, the water goddess, before adding a small drop of my blood to the water. In doing so I return to her the two fluids of life as I empty the bowl.

So far this second life has been good. But as Adagouti knows, the money left in the back of the sleeping room closet by the late Tomaso Akriki will not last indefinitely. And without that, how will I afford such things as my weekly housekeeper? Or Marzouk, come to that?

As I walk into the kitchen and dining area, I am still amazed by what I've been told is a calendar on the wall. Marzouk has crossed off another square, indicating that today is Tuesday, March 4th, 1969.

He greets me with, "Good morning, Sayidi." Then puts a bowl of fresh cut bread on the table, followed by two plates of khlea and eggs, scrambled the American way, or so he assures me. I sip my tea, take a piece of bread, and start to eat.

After a silent five minutes, Marzouk asks, "Forgive me, but is everything okay with you, Sayidi? You appear tense – stressed even. I take it you slept well?"

"I slept. But all it confirmed was that I should be wary of a nearby leopard."

Marzouk becomes slightly agitated. "You are talking about a dream, aren't you, Sayidi? As far as I know, Ekpe has been outlawed for some time."

I look up from my breakfast. "I'm talking about Death herself, alsinijab alsaghir. What's this Ekpe?"

"A disbanded and condemned secret leopard cult that practiced murder, so it could indulge in cannibalism, Sayidi."

I smile and take another piece of bread. "Sadly, that might be preferable to wondering when Death will strike her bargain with the Gods, then take me by surprise."

Marzouk takes another piece of bread before casually continuing the conversation.

"To be forever looking over your shoulder cannot be good for your health. What you need, Sayidi, is a relaxing shave and a haircut – 20 fils."

"And for that price the service is good?"

"The place I always recommended to my passengers is in the Turkish district. Mehmet Jakar is the finest barber, shaver, and Indian head masseuse, in the whole of this city."

"And you use him yourself?"

"Alas Sayidi, would that I could afford such a regular luxury. But if I could, then most certainly I'd visit him should I have need of his services."

I look closely at Marzouk, unable to tell if he speaks the truth, or lies as fluently as a member of the city's legal profession. I say, "Would I be able to get an appointment to be ministered to by one so famous?"

Marzouk smiles, "A word from me and he would refuse the king himself."

2

After a twenty minute journey of barely missed collisions and several hand gestures I've not seen before, Marzouk parks up alongside a single storey barber's shop in what appears to be a backstreet, off the main souk, in the Turkish district of the city. As he drives off in a haze of exhaust smoke, he calls out, "I'll be back in an hour, Sayidi."

Five minutes later I am in the large chrome and black leather chair, tilted backwards, face wrapped in hot towels. The air smells of bay rum, cloves, cigars and pomade. On one side I can hear Mehmet as he strops a razor. From the other the noise of the street outside through the open doorway. A brown Bakelite radio on the windowsill is powered from the same light socket as the hair clippers. From the speaker comes the BBC World Service at a low volume.

Behind me I hear a rustle as someone enters and sits on one of several chairs against the back wall. Moments later a woman's voice asks, "Are you Tomaso Memindip, the private detective who was in the newspapers recently? You solved a murder before the police did."

Mehmet removes the towel covering my mouth, then goes back to slowly stropping the razor.

Cautious, I say, "Yes, I'm that Tomaso Memindip."

After a decision-making hesitation, she continues with the conversation. "My name is Anita Purkell. I believe my brother, Dante, is missing. I want you to find him."

I fold the towel away from my eyes. The large mirror in front of me reflects a young woman – maybe 25 or 26? – light brown hair and European complexion rather than Afrikaans, her accent tinged with Northern Italian. She's wearing a silk headscarf of watercolour poppies on a milk cream background, the design out-shining her light cotton dress – though her eyes are hidden behind round blind-beggar sunglasses.

Mehmet removes the remaining towels, and before he coats my face with shaving soap, I ask, "How do you know he's missing? Have you talked to the police? Hospitals? Other members of your family? Has he perhaps been declared a dissident and is hiding from the militia?"

Having worked the soap up into a lather, Mehmet deftly coats my cheeks, chin and neck with foam, before picking up the cutthroat razor and scraping it off with the newly honed blade.

As he shaves me, Ms Purkell continues, "I've already checked the hospitals for the last week. The police? They've shown no interest in looking into his disappearance. So when a taxi driver handed me your card, I decided to see if you could help. To answer your last question, my brother isn't an activist. He has no interest in politics."

"A taxi driver?" As best I remember, Marzouk had retired his permit when he became my assistant.

"Yes, White Knight Cabs. He said he worked for a member of your agency. Marzouk something-or-other."

"So how did you know where to find me?"

"The driver said you'd be here before ten today for your regular hot towel and massage. If I needed something solving, then I should talk to you. I visited the library first thing this morning, read about you in the newspapers, and thought you might be able to help me." She pauses and wrinkles her nose. "If you're not interested then I'll try and find someone else."

As she starts to leave, I remember Adagouti's words about staying in the favour of the Gods. "I haven't said I'll not take your case."

"So you will?"

"I'll need more details before I decide. And we need to discuss my fee…."

She sits back down again. "I'm not sure what happened. We used to be so close, but something's changed. He became furtive – secretive – and nervous. Then I received a letter saying he needed to go away for a while – some kind of large project that required his full attention. But to just leave without talking to me first is something he'd never do. That's how I knew something was wrong."

"Did the letter say where he was going?"

"No. Just that the only way he could concentrate was through total isolation."

Mehmet finishes my shave, wipes away the excess soap, then picks up the electric clippers. "Trim? It's an all in price."

"No, this is more than enough." I get up and look directly at Ms Purkell. "You have the card from the taxi driver?" She nods, and hands it to me. It looks almost identical to the ones I carry – except in place of my name is The Fourth Floor Detective Agency. I hand it back to her. "If you could visit my, er, office? Say 3pm this afternoon?"

"Whatever. I just want to find Dante. Or at least know he's safe and well."

I watch her go, then turn to Mehmet. "I understand you do the relaxing head massage?"

The barber nods and smiles, flexing and cracking his fingers.

I get back in the chair. "Ten minutes. Then I have a little squirrel to skin."

3

Across the dining table, Marzouk says, "But, Sayidi, how are we going to get people to come to us if we don't advertise?" He has a point, but I don't want to concede it.

I look at the clock - ten to 3 - then at Marzouk. "We'll discuss this matter later, but for now what've you learned about this Anita Purkell?"

"She works for Laverne and Maples, a legal firm dealing exclusively with International import and export. She's their translator – Arabic, French, English – contracts, licences, that sort of thing."

"So she is someone of importance?"

"You'd think, as their chief translator and transcriber, but her clothing says otherwise. Not short of money, but frugal."

I remember her appearance earlier. Quality silk headscarf, but cheaper cotton frock. "And her brother?"

"Alas, Sayidi, none of the drivers know anything about him. If he takes taxis then they're not from the White Knight Company."

I look at Marzouk incredulously. "They're your source of information?"

"A very reliable source. People talk to drivers, and drivers remember details that passengers believe to be inconsequential."

"And do you gossip about me?"

"Sayidi, please. We are the Fourth Floor Detective Agency. Information is our business."

"Which is another thing -" There is a knock on the door "- that we will need to discuss later. Go, welcome Miss Purkell."

<h1 style="text-align:center">4</h1>

Anita Purkell sits back in the Colonial club style chair. "No, I didn't save the envelope, so I've no idea what the postmark was."

We're in the living room at the back of the apartment. Large sliding glass doors leading out onto the balcony face two comfortable chairs and a sofa, so occupants can see across part of the city. While Marzouk prepares tea, I sit in the other single chair and ask some questions.

"The letter mentions a project? What does your brother do?"

"He's a printer and book binder by trade. Sometimes he helps with restoration and preservation projects for libraries and the like. That's when his assistant takes over, so he can concentrate on whatever he needs to. But when I asked, Constantine says he had no idea that Dante had taken on another contract. He'd found a note two weeks ago, pushed under the shop door. It was similar to the letter. An additional contract that would take up all of his time, and that he trusted Constantine to complete and finish off any outstanding work on the order book. That's why the police are disinterested. They took the letter and note at face value, which is why they don't believe me."

I make a pretence of mulling things over, then, "Okay, 500 dirham a week, plus expenses. And that doesn't guarantee success. I'll also need the address of your brother's business."

She opens her shoulder bag and removes 5 notes from a small roll. "I just want to know he's safe and well." Small notebook and slim gold pencil provides the address. "Constantine lives above the shop and often works late to clear any backlog." She looks at me as Marzouk brings tea. Once poured, she asks, "Do you need anything else?"

"Only a photograph of your brother."

She delves back into her bag and presents me with a passport and an expired travel document. "These are the best I could find at short notice."

She sips tea as I look at the small monochrome picture stapled to the visa before passing the paperwork over to Marzouk. A young man, early 30s, dark black hair, bright intelligent eyes, goatee beard. Marzouk carefully removes the staples. "This should be adequate for our purposes. I assume he still has the beard?"

Ms Purkell smiles. "Yes. Despite my comments, he's still

kept it."

Then we both rise and go to the front door, which Marzouk opens ahead of us. As she leaves, she turns. "I have a terrible feeling he's in some kind of trouble."

I smile to try and calm her. "We shall see what we shall see."

5

The following day, after breakfast and an unnervingly uneventful journey across the city, Marzouk drops me off at Kitab Tabiea, Dante's business address. I tell Marzouk to wait, and when I enter the print shop I'm greeted by tall, stocky Constantine. He is an old Greek in his fifties– neck like a bull and dark eyes, deeper than a man's soul. His hands look like they have splashes of black ink forever ingrained under the skin.

I shake his hand, saying, "I am Tomaso Memindip," as I pass him one of my cards.

"Coffee?" He indicates a stainless steel electric percolator to the side of an old floor standing printing press.

"Thank you, yes."

As he pours two cups I move a pile of untrimmed handbills from a chair seat and sit by his workbench-cum-desk.

He adds sugar and as he brings it over, I say, "I'm searching for Dante Purkell. I've been asked to look into his disappearance."

"I know. Anita told me last night. But according to the police he's not missing."

"And you?"

"Maybe. Maybe not. The letter and note could be forged, or he just had a bad day working on some difficult engraving, or woodcut, and his hands were hurting from too much tool work."

I look over the workbench. "So if he has a new job, where does he work? Obviously not here."

"We can't store chemicals in the shop – not even in a locked cabinet. The city's worried in case they can be used for bomb making. Maybe, if you were a knowledgeable chemist and had a secret laboratory." He shakes his head dismissively. "The gendarmes search us regularly. They also check everything we print, in case we're stupid enough to run off a thousand copies of some political manifesto, and keep them here on show. Dante has his own workshop, about half way between here and Fehmal. Head towards there and you can't miss it. It's built out of the remains of the old Legion outpost. Dante has it on a long term lease."

I look at him and take a gamble. "And did you find anything when you were last there?"

He smiles. "You're sharp. After Anita visited a week ago I took a trip up there. It looked like it had been searched, but whoever had done the searching had been careful not to leave the workshop in a state. Dante is very particular about his tools, and to me it was obvious they had been disturbed. I could tell as someone had put them back in the wrong order. Plus," He opens a drawer in the bench. "There were these papers in a makeshift fire. Dante would never burn anything in the workshop in case the smoke got into the book he was working on."

Constantine hands me several pieces of quality writing

paper, one with a printed address above a typewritten letter – the address, scorched, but unburned, The Museum of Antiquities. Some of the pieces have large smears of what looks like a heavy yellowish oil – slightly sticky, and not absorbed well by the paper.

He goes back to the percolator and refills his cup. "I've told no one about them. After I took them I thought better of it, but didn't want to be caught putting them back. You can keep them, if you think they'll do you any good. Oh, and when you find Dante? Tell him he now owes me for six weeks work."

I pick up an envelope from the bench and slip the half burned pieces into it. As I start to leave, I ask, "Do I need a key?"

"Side windowsill, third flowerpot from the left."

Back in the Chrysler, Marzouk is eager for excitement. "Where to now, Sayidi?"

I pause, then decide that Dante's workshop can wait. "I need to go to the Museum of Antiquities. How soon do you think you can get us there?"

Marzouk looks at his newly purchased wristwatch, and I wonder if 100 dirham a month is perhaps an overly generous salary. "Ten, maybe fifteen minutes."

"Then let's get going before the sun becomes unbearable."

"Right, Sayidi, the museum it is!" And with a twist of the steering wheel we are back into the chaos that is the city's traffic system.

6

The Museum is an oasis of cool marble and overhead fans –

several Egyptian statues grace the sides of the double height entrance hall, which is busy with tourists sightseeing and workmen putting up large pin boards and posters advertising an up-coming exhibition. Central to the area is a large circular desk with Information written on a sign hanging above it.

As I step up to the counter, an attentive young woman smiles, and asks, "How can we help you today?" Definitely not a local official.

"I'd like to see," I look at the name I've written on the back of the envelope – silently blaming Marzouk's driving for my inabilities with writing implements. "Doctor Keyatta. I'm trying to trace someone he wrote to recently."

She turns and points to a tall man standing near a set of stairs leading to the next floor. "He's over there, organising the new display. On Saturday an original copy of the Shahnameh will be on view. It's one of only five copies known to have survived from the 11th Century."

I head towards the person indicated, saying, "Thank you, I'll endeavour to ask of it when we speak."

Engrossed in his work, Keyatta's dark skin is emphasised by his white shirt and light fawn trousers – and he appears overly tall to those around him. Zulu origins perhaps?

Keyatta looks up as I approach. "I need more pin boards. We're trying to make this an event not to be missed, but…." His voice tails off as he realises his mistake.

I clear my throat. "I am the detective Tomaso Memindip, and I'd like to discuss the disappearance of Dante Purkell," I hold up the envelope, "And why someone would wish to burn a letter with your signature on it."

"Disappearance? We still need two more posters for the Shahnameh display." He takes the envelope from me, lifts the flap and looks at the half burned papers. "This is the work order for those pieces. Six large black and white posters of the Shahnameh, open at an illuminated page, and the artwork hand coloured so that it stands out. Eye catching." He puts the damaged papers into the envelope and hands it back to me.

I push the conversation forward. "When did Dante deliver the last one?"

"The order is for six in total, but we only received the fourth one several days ago. Dante's helper – the Greek – he delivers them."

I look at the 4 foot high poster to the side of a large empty glass cabinet. Soft focus black and white, with the pages of the open book a bright splash of multi-coloured detail. Across the top if it are the words:

The Persians – An Historical Retrospective

As I study it, impressed by the beauty of the artwork, Keyatta says:

"We took our copy of the Shahnameh to the National Museum in Cairo, and they verified my authentication as correct. It's from the original copy studio that Ferdowsi used to publish his epic poem. Fifty thousand distichs." He looks at me enquiringly, then adds "Couplets. Two line verses?"

I don't mention that I remember hearing a travelling Storyman recite sections of it, one evening, around a large fire which, according to Adagouti, was on the evening of June 18th, 1693. Instead I just nod and smile.

Keyatta continues, "The exhibition opens with a special

preview on Friday, which gives us just today and tomorrow to get the posters and put them in the right places. At this rate we'll be working well into Friday morning. Will you be coming to the opening?"

I shake my head. "I'm committed to this investigation."

Keyatta carefully looks about us, then says, "Would you care to see the Shahnameh before we put it into the display case?"

"Is such possible?"

"For a relatively small donation – to the Museum, of course."

I take a 20 dirham note from my wallet. Keyatta silently looks at it, then up at me, his hands still by his sides. I reach back in and add another 20, to which he smiles, folds the money into his trouser pocket, and leads the way back to his office.

Closing the door behind us, he moves to a large safe set in the back wall. As he spins the combination dial, he says, "I have it here. We needed it out of the vault so it could be photographed, and then taken to Cairo for authentication."

"But you were sure it was an original before then?"

"Of course. I authenticated it myself after I discovered it in one of the old vault storage boxes."

From inside the safe he takes out a pair of white cotton gloves and puts them on before removing the bound work. Carefully he places it on the blotter of his desk and starts opening it at various bookmarked pages.

The illustrations are breath-taking – their quality and colours powerful enough to snare the viewer into looking deeper, discovering detail that would be missed by a casual glance. Keyatta turns to another section, and we are transported from the court of Hushang to the exploits of Kai Khosrow.

Keyatta says, "The poet died almost penniless, having lost the support of his patron and benefactor over religious beliefs." He closes the book, puts it back in the safe with the white gloves, and re-spins the dial. Security done, he escorts me back to the Information desk.

"Should you visit the museum on Friday for the preview opening, you'll find a lot more unique and wonderful items included in the exhibition. And if you cannot make it for the preview, then the pieces will be on show for the next 4 weeks."

"Thank you. I shall endeavour to visit if I can." Then I head out, passing between the giant Egyptian statues and into the late morning sunlight.

7

As I walk down the Museum steps towards Marzouk and his taxi, a booming voice behind me calls out, "Hey, Mr. Investigator, what're you doing here?"

Commandant Monnes, camel-coloured uniform sharply pressed, Sam Brown holster at his hip, comes down the steps towards me. "What are you and your little squirrel up to? And don't give me any of that righter of wrongs either. I now know all about the 4th Floor Detective Agency."

I smile a greeting. "At present I am tasked to find a missing person. Dante Purkell." I pause to see if Monnes reacts to the name. He remains unresponsive, so I continue. "His sister has concerns about his welfare."

"And your business brought you here?"

I open the envelope and show him the oil-stained and charred remains of the letter. "His assistant found this part burned when he was at their workshop near Fehmal. I wanted to talk to Doctor Keyatta about what the letter may have contained. He says it was for work printing and hand colouring posters for the upcoming display."

"The Shahnameh? My men and I have been run ragged checking and rechecking the security for this event."

"And you're sure the Shahnameh will be safe?"

Monnes glares at me. "Of course I'm sure." A short pause, then "Why? What do you know?"

I hold up my hands. "Nothing, I swear."

Monnes half smiles. "I doubt I'd believe you even if you did take an oath. Have you found anything else?"

"Nothing besides the half-burned letter."

"Well, it wasn't there when my gendarmes visited his workshop about two weeks ago."

I try not to sound surprised. "I was given it by Dante's assistant, Constantine. He said he found it the day after Dante's disappearance." I take a quick breath and see if he will talk more about the case. "His sister said you'd shown no interest."

"Actually she's his half-sister – different mothers. She came to us and due to the Shahnameh connection I had two of my men do a discrete investigation. They found nothing untoward." Monnes holds out his hand, and I reluctantly give him the envelope as he asks, "Any more evidence you're withholding?"

I smile. "It's only evidence if there's been a crime committed." He glares at me, so I quickly add, "None as yet."

"Let's keep it that way." Then he carries on down the steps, pauses to glare at Marzouk in his taxi, before waving his arms and moving him on.

Two minutes later, after Marzouk has gone round the block, he parks back up alongside the museum steps.

"Where to now, Sayidi?"

"I think it's time to visit Dante's workshop."

8

The ride out is fairly uneventful, due to the lack of any oncoming traffic, and the fact it is getting too near midday to make long distance travel anything but uncomfortable. Down a dusty side road we come to what looks like an old single storey building of clay and daub – whitewashed walls and flat roof to keep the heat down. The wind powered water pump is static, but the sound of a generator at the back of the property is loud enough to indicate someone is at home. That, and the 1957 Ford pick-up truck parked outside.

Marzouk gets out, softly walks up to one of the front windows and takes a discrete look inside. Satisfied, he returns to the car.

"Well, Sayidi, it is not quite as we would've hoped."

"I take it Dante Purcell is not to be seen?"

"I saw only the big Greek. He seems to be working on something spread across a large draftsman's board. It looks like he's painting something."

"And no one else?"

"With the amount of benches and equipment, it would be hard for anyone not to be noticed."

"Still, let us both see what Constantine has to say for himself."

As quietly as possible I get out of the car and we walk up to the front door, Marzouk leading, his hand in his jacket pocket where I know he keeps a flick knife. When we reach the entrance, Marzouk moves to one side and I take hold of the door handle. I mentally prepare myself, then turn the handle. But instead of the expected resistance there isn't any, and I stumble through the doorway, almost tripping over the threshold board.

Startled by our entrance, Constantine exclaims, "Chazos!" before catching his breath, then adds, "Why didn't you just knock like normal people?" He waves a hand at the massive black and white poster he's been working on. "Now I've got to clean the oil paint off and re-do that section. It's bad enough I'm having to finish these two and get them dried before tomorrow morning, without the likes of you and your sidekick scaring the Devil out of me. What do you want anyway?"

Marzouk remains silent while I explain. "We have come from the Museum of Antiquities, so we know you've been delivering the posters to Dr Keyatta. But when I spoke to you at the shop in the city, you said Dante had taken the project on himself, using this workshop to complete the order. And here we are, finding that it's you who has been doing the work all along."

Constantine sits back on the draftsman's high stool, and

puts the fine haired brush to one side. "Dante did the original research. He took all the photos, sourced the pigments and researched the old Persian methods for creating inks and illustration techniques. Me? I'm the one who gets dressed in leather aprons and heavy rubber gloves when it comes to developing photographic negatives and creating the metal etchings. Only in this case I didn't have to. Multiple screen prints, various coloured layers from black, through grey, to a very thin white overlay."

It's clear he's a craftsman who is passionate about his skills.

"So what happened to Dante?"

The Greek sighs. "I told you, I don't know. One day he's here discussing the project. Then he talks to his sister, and the next thing I know he's nowhere to be found."

"Do you know what they talked about? Did they quarrel?"

He sucks on a tooth, then, "I'm not really sure. They both went down into the cellar – it's where we keep acids, thinners, base paint oils – so I didn't hear anything. And when they came back up they were both silent. She left immediately. Dante showed me some of the photographs he'd taken at the museum, said he intended to colour the posters using oils, then left without saying where he was going."

"So who tried to burn the letter?"

"No idea. I locked up one evening, came back two days later and the half burned papers were on top of the carving bench, scattered with wood shavings and a pool of boiled linseed oil, all stone cold. Dante would never damage the bench doing something like that, plus boiled oil rarely ignites without some considerable heating first."

"And the spare key?"

"Still under the plant pot on the sill. It's not exactly a secret hiding place."

"And does Doctor Keyatta know it's you completing the work?"

"Probably not. All he cares about is the up-coming exhibition." He looks up at the clock on the far wall. "Now, if you're done, I've this poster to fix and spread on the drying frame outside. The midday sun gives the work the appearance of age – which is what Keyatta wants."

Marzouk is already heading towards the car when I turn and ask Constantine, "With Dante missing, who will Keyatta pay for the work?"

"Anita. She deals with that side of the business."

"So she has more concerns than just a missing brother?"

"Maybe. But that's a question you're going to have to ask her yourself. Now, if you don't mind?"

I nod my goodbye, and once in the back of the car I tell Marzouk, "Head back to the manzil. The sun is at midday, and neither of us are English."

He throws the car into gear, stamps down on the accelerator, and leaving a cloud of dust and the rattle of small stones behind us, we depart.

Back on the main road again, he asks, "What are your feelings about all of this, Sayidi?"

"I think something isn't right when Constantine is completing work and Dante is nowhere to be seen. I think it's time to talk to Ms Purkell again – but that will be after the heat is out of the day."

9

After a restful, Adagouti-free nap, I eventually retire to the living room. Looking out across part of the city, I am sitting with the telephone handset pressed against my ear. The secretary at Laverne & Maples has gone to check on whether Ms Purkell is at her desk, or away somewhere, though not before telling me that:

"She is an important person. She's always very busy and might not want to be disturbed." Then she adds, emphatically, "By anyone."

After several minutes, the secretary's voice comes back on the line. "Please wait while I connect you."

There is a loud click, an insistent buzzing like an angry bee, then Ms Purkell picks up the receiver.

"You have news?" Her voice sounds cold, though I've yet to get used to this impersonal form of communication.

"Not in regard to Dante, but I do have some questions that require answering." There's silence in my ear, so I continue. "Why didn't you tell me Dante is your step-brother?"

"Would it have made any difference?"

"No. But it would have been nice if you'd been honest with me from the start. Especially when I find out it's you who issues and clears the invoices for your brother's company."

"I don't see – "

I cut her off. "I'm assuming you need him to countersign bank drafts and cheques?"

"Yes, but – "

"So this is about Constantine's back wages?"

"No. I mean yes. Sort of. I need to transfer some funds in regard to several items Dante was commissioned to create and export. If they're stuck in the Freeport holding area then the buyers will demand their money back."

"And these items are?"

She hesitates, then says, "They are two facsimiles of the Shahnameh. Dante was allowed to take photographs of the original, but instead of taking a few, he took photographs of every page. He wasn't intending to sell the facsimiles as originals. He just created three. One for the Museum of Antiquities, and two others for private collectors of Persian literature. Those are the two which are held in the Freeport warehouse, in storage, waiting for him to sign the release papers."

"Who else knows about the copies?"

"Just us, as far as I know. The museum wouldn't be at all happy knowing what Dante's done. They've had their copy authenticated, but if word were to get out that it was their copy that's been copied, then I don't think they'd look to employ him on any more of their projects."

"And the buyers know they're purchasing copies, and not the real thing?"

She doesn't hesitate this time. "Yes! They knew from the start, when they commissioned them. I made sure that Dante had paperwork to that effect, just in case something went wrong and he was accused of forgery."

"And the copies? They're still in the holding shed?"

"Why shouldn't they be? No one has paid for their release or onward delivery. Until that's done then they're stuck there."

"And you still have no idea of where your stepbrother might be?"

She pauses, and when she speaks I can hear the emotion in her voice rather than the cold anger of frustration.

"Despite our differences he is still family. And that is something which is important to me."

"Above all else?"

There's another few seconds of thoughtful hesitation, then, "Yes. I cannot think of anything that would make me believe otherwise."

I say "Thank you," then put the handset back in its cradle, all the time trying to work out why I now feel uneasy at the way things are progressing.

10

As the Greenwich Time Signal peeps its last 'peeeeeep' from the speaker of the radiogram – indicating that it is now 10am, local time, Thursday March 6th, precisely – there is a knock at the front door of the manzil.

I wait for Marzouk to answer it, but on the third, more insistent series of thumps, I realise that Marzouk is still out on an errand.

I turn off the radio, calling out "I'm coming! Akbh jamah nafsak!" And when I open the front door, I'm greeted by the young gendarme I now know is called Nadeem Maleek. He smiles a weary smile.

"If I had any horses to hold, Mr Investigator, then I would hope they'd all be thoroughbreds."

I smile. Despite the young man's chosen profession, I still find myself liking him. Nodding a greeting, I ask, "I have tea on the stove, or is this more a business call?"

"Alas it is all business these days. Commandant Monnes requests the displeasure of your company in regard to a matter you are apparently involved in."

"Dante Purkell?"

He holds his hands up. "I am but the messenger, recounting words and instructions that were passed on to me." He purses his lips, then continues, "Needless to say he is not best pleased." He looks over my shoulder – both the left and then the right – before observing: "I'm assuming you'll require transport? I have a car waiting in the street below."

I write a quick message for Marzouk to read on his return, then accompany gendarme Maleek to the police station – a car journey remarkable for its total lack of any interruption or confrontational incident. So remarkable is it that, as we pull up outside Police HQ, I make a mental note to ask Marzouk about getting his car fitted with a siren and flashing lights – an addition I truly believe would be life-saving. Namely my own.

Inside I barely have time to announce myself "Tomaso Memindip, to see –" before the desk sergeant cuts me off with a curt "You. Wait. Over there." He then picks up the telephone, presses a button on the console below, waits, then says, "Your suspect is here, Commandant. Do you want to interview him in your office or in the cells?"

Before I have a chance to splutter my indignation, the sergeant says, "Very good, sir." He puts the phone down and points to me again. "You. Commandant's office. Third door down. You can count that far, can't you?"

I smile politely, enquire in old Berber Tamazight if he is the result of his father having had congress with livestock rather than one of his wives, and then proceed quickly down the passageway until I am in front of Commandant Monnes' office door. Before I can respectfully knock, I hear a shouted, "Get in here!"

I open the office door, dreading the fires of damnation, and am ordered to "Sit!" It appears there is a moratorium on the police speaking words of more than one syllable.

On his desk, illuminated by the large, brass, swan neck desk lamp, is an open folder. Inside its covers are the pieces of the partially burned letter from Doctor Keyatta.

Without looking at me, Monnes asks, "Is the blood on this anything to do with you?"

Caught by surprise I answer honestly, "No. Why should I have bled on it and not mentioned the fact when I handed the pieces over?"

Monnes looks up at me and I hold his stare unblinkingly, as I would when facing down a cobra. Eventually he looks away.

"My forensic team found traces of blood preserved under the linseed oil. The only thing they can deduce is that it's blood. The damage from the oil is pretty extensive, but they're sure it's blood."

"Has Doctor Keyatta claimed ownership?" Clearly not, otherwise why call me to his office.

"Nobody is claiming it as theirs. Not the Doctor or his secretary, nor the Greek, and now you."

"So you're concluding that it belongs to Dante Purkell?"

"I conclude nothing until I have hard evidence – or at least a body, and a suspect to match it to. However, my instincts tell me that the blood may well be that of Dante Purkell, and the letter was set alight by his killer."

"That then asks the question; why add linseed oil?"

Monnes rubs at his eyes with the knuckles of his index fingers. "I think the plan was to burn the workshop to the ground. Only whoever attempted to do it was too stupid to know that boiled Linseed oil needs to be heated to a high temperature before it will catch alight. That rules out Dante himself and the Greek as well."

Monnes looks at me sharply. "You don't happen to know what the properties of linseed oil are, do you?"

I adopt my cobra killing stare once more. "Actually I do," but leave out the part about only recently learning it from Constantine the Greek. "But that aside, why would Dante Purkell, or Constantine, want to burn down their only source of income?"

Monnes barks a short "Ha!" followed by, "Not for the insurance, that's for sure. They don't have any."

"And you think the blood is from Dante Purkell's death?"

"No body, no murder. And no murderer either. I'm waiting to see if they still have the corpse dog over at the station in Rondehal. I think the Red Cross left one the last time they had a bomb take out a building. Either that, or the gendarmes have eaten the poor animal. Regardless, I'll requisition it and have some of my men check out the ground around that desert workshop of theirs. Half the time the wind changes everything. Footprints disappear, sand covers stones, everything becomes as smooth and perfect as the skin of an apricot. But the scent of death is something else entirely."

"Be'kal's breath can be both a blessing, and a curse at times."

Commandant Monnes looks at me sharply. "You don't strike me as a follower of the ancient beliefs."

"I, er... I've been researching my ancestral line. Psylli, I believe, before the time of the Muslim invasions. Be'kal is one of the Old Gods, from a time now lost and all but forgotten."

Monnes, still glaring at me, says, "Well, don't go muttering that sort of thing in public. There are imans and fanatics who don't take kindly to such. And the last thing I need is some kind of religious uprising. It's bad enough with all the Communists and politicos agitating things, but religion is something else entirely."

Monnes looks back down at the documents on his desk, and without looking up, says, "If you're not gone from this building in the next 60 seconds, I'll charge you with loitering."

Outside, and nearing midday, I'm thankful to see that Marzouk is parked as discretely as he can across the main road, in the shade of the adjacent building.

As I settle in the back seat, I ask: "Did you get my message?"

"Yes, Sayidi. And I have news. There were originally two items crated up for export, as you rightly believed. However, three weeks ago one was removed and replaced by another of identical proportions, with no change to the despatch or delivery arrangements. The two crates are being held on one docket at the Departures warehouse until the administration fees and storage costs have been met. Until then they remain in bond, under lock and key."

"And if the fees are not paid on time?"

"Then the goods become forfeit, and will be disposed of via public auction at the end of the relevant month."

"Fine." I consider our next course of action, finally deciding, "It's too close to midday to worry about anything other than getting back to the manzil before the sun bakes us to a crisp. But first thing this afternoon I feel it would be prudent to talk to Dr Keyatta once more."

11

"Doctor Keyatta is very, very, busy and cannot be disturbed." The receptionist is very insistent on the latter as she looks down her nose at me from the safety of her Information Desk barrier. Behind me a line of people has started to form, some checking their watches, others grumbling to themselves about this unexpected delay.

Unperturbed, I continue with my line of questioning. "So he is here?"

"Of course he's here. We are due to have the exhibition preview start at 6pm tomorrow, so these final 24 hours are vitally important in getting things perfect. We're expecting many civil dignitaries, plus the backers, obviously, and other very important people." Again she looks down her nose at me. "People who are more important than mere investigators."

"Perfectly understandable," I try and smile as sincerely as I can while wondering if another 20 dirham donation to

Museum funds might be called for. Her stern expression dismisses the idea for me, so I resort to other tactics. Looking over her shoulder I smile and wave as if seeing someone I recognise, and when she turns to see who it might be, I slip around the desk and behind one of the Egyptian statues, heading into the inner sanctum of the Museum itself.

As she turns back she is confronted by the next angry person in search of an answer to their enquiry.

I carry on down the passageway until I locate Doctor Keyatta's office door. Without knocking I enter, surprising him sitting at his desk, safe open behind him, and with the copy of the Shahnameh open on his desk. The binding is of worn and cracked leather, most probably from an old and inconsequential volume picked up in a backstreet souk. The pages have been warped along their exposed edges, and coloured a light coffee brown. The Greek's words come back to me regarding the effects of the sun.

Keyatta stand up, obviously angry, but I pre-empt his protests by saying, "You must be disappointed that the posters have flaws in them."

"Flaws?" Thrown off guard, he sounds confused and indignant. "What flaws can there be? They look perfectly okay to a trained, as opposed to an uneducated, eye."

I shake my head. "No. The posters show the original damages caused by time. You can recreate the appearance of age, but you cannot replicate it completely. Plus I don't think it was Dante Purkell's intension to deceive, nor to steal the original. The breath of Be'kal may well smooth away imperfections in the sand, but it cannot replace photographic images." Without pausing, I then ask: "Where did you hide

Dante Purkell's body?"

"What?"

"You had to move his body when the desert workshop didn't catch fire and burn down. I'm assuming you panicked when the oil didn't catch alight, leaving you with all that mess."

Keyatta's expression becomes cold as he slowly sits back down again. "I should've persevered and gone looking for something more flammable. But the wind had started to get up and there had been warnings of a heavy sandstorm travelling southward. I didn't want to get caught in that. It would've choked the car's engine and left me stranded. But I'd already dragged his body from the drying racks out the back, so I was left with no other option but to change my plan."

"But why did you kill him? A falling out of thieves?"

Keyatta smiles. "Oh no, nothing as stupid as that. Dante was far too honest to be a thief. Proud and arrogant, yes. But greed certainly got the better of him. When I approached him to create a copy I used the excuse that the Museum would keep the original in the vault and display the copy, which is true – the insurance company would never allow the original to be displayed without armed guards protecting it. I'd even agreed to put a note beside it to that effect, and naming Dante as the creator of the facsimile. All good publicity." He picks up an ornate letter opener from the cluttered desktop blotter, turning it over in his hands and looking down at it as if fascinated by it. "But Dante didn't follow instructions. Instead of creating one he created three."

"Who were the other two copies for?"

"I don't know. From the addresses on the packing cases I assume they were for dealers or specific collectors. He'd even included some extra text at the bottom of the pages, close to the spine. It said something like 'This is a facsimile created with permission' then named me. The third copy had that text masked out – apparently something that's easy to do during the screen printing process."

"So you buried his body elsewhere?"

Keyatta sighs. "I didn't have time to create a funeral pyre. There's an old waddi on the way back to the city – usually full of scavengers. About a mile up it there's the remains of a cave. I dumped his body in that. When the waters come he'll be covered in silt. If not, then he's probably kept a Fennec or a sand cat and her cubs fed for several weeks."

As I see the flick of his wrist I'm already stepping to one side and the letter opener sticks firmly into the wood of the door frame with a thud barely audible above the outside noise.

Keyatta sighs again and shrugs his shoulders. "Well, you cannot blame a man for trying. So, where do we go from here? I assume you either want to be paid to keep quiet, or you're looking for a cut of the sale when I make it?"

"Is that what you would do if you were me?"

"No. If I were you, then I'd kill me and take 100 percent."

"But that only works if I already know where to sell it and what price I should be asking. You created a problem by killing Dante Purkell. You need his signature to release the two crates – one of which I'm sure now contains the museum's copy of the Shahnameh. I suspect you've been trying to practice his signature? It's a shame that his half-sister, Anita, completed and signed most of the letters and all of the invoices. I'm assuming it was you who forged the letter to her and the note pushed under the shop door?"

"I managed to razor a page of his handwriting from the front of his work book, which was all I could find after the fire didn't take. It was a rushed job, but it seemed to work after a fashion." Keyatta looks at the various ornaments and accessories on the desk that are within easy reach. Nothing with any point or blade, though a statue of a horned representation of the god, Isis, strikes me as having potential if used in close combat. Keyatta stands, snatches up a round glass paperweight and is about to throw it when the resonant voice and body of Commandant Monnes, barges through the half open door and I have to jump to one side to avoid being caught by the door handle.

"I wouldn't do that if I were you, Doctor. It'll only add to the already long list of charges you'll be facing in court."

Keyatta, looking crestfallen and dejected, sits back down before two burly gendarmes enter and drag him out of his office in handcuffs.

Monnes sits down in one of the comfortable chairs half facing the desk.

"Your little rat is a persistent creature, I'll give him that."

"You mean Marzouk?"

"How many other rodents do you have that do your bidding?"

"None. Marzouk is more than efficient to be sufficient."

"Whatever. I also sent two men down to the dockyard. Apparently the security guards were initially a little reluctant about letting them have the two cases until it was pointed out what they were involved in, albeit indirectly."

"So how much did you manage to hear?"

"Almost all, I think. At least the most important part, where he admitted to killing Dante Purkell and hiding his corpse up a waddi."

I look at the doorframe, still with the letter opener sticking from it. "Was that before or after the attempted murder?"

"Hard to tell. Probably after, I would say." He cocks his head a little to one side. "You may think it attempted murder. Others might believe it to be justifiable homicide." He stands, straightens his light brown uniform, and is about to leave when the noise from the corridor outside the office manifests itself in the form of the woman who was behind the Information Desk in the foyer.

"Tell me what is going on! I've just seen Doctor Keyatta being escorted out of the building in handcuffs!"

Monnes glares her into silence. "He's being arrested and charged with murder, along with fraud and grand theft for good measure."

"But what do we do about the exhibition?"

Monnes impatiently adjusts the gun in its holster. "Madam, I wouldn't look on these events as some kind of loss. Take this as a promotional opportunity."

"What?"

"From now on you're in charge of it all." With that he departs the office, no doubt heading back to the Police HQ, leaving the poor woman even more confused. She turns to me, but all I can do is shrug my shoulders, smile, and make good my escape back out into the street.

12

As I put the telephone receiver back onto its cradle, Marzouk asks:

"It is never a pleasant task, Sayidi, to tell a person that a loved one is no more. How did Miss Purkell take the news of her stepbrother's death?"

The coldness in her voice had been obvious. I was simply confirming what she already believed to be true. The Commandant's gendarmes had still to locate Dante Purkell's remains, at which time they would inform her, and the world, of his official demise. But for now she had a chance to prepare herself for the inevitable onslaught of prying reporters and staff photographers. They'd already had the double feeding frenzy of both the attempted theft of an artefact of great importance, but also the downfall of a very prominent public official in the form of Doctor Keyatta. Now it was a case of which publication could out sensationalise the others, their front pages vying for public attention. Anything as long as it extracted the fils from the readers' pockets.

"She seems to be taking it very well, considering the circumstances."

Marzouk looks thoughtful for a moment. "So, with the original poems back at the Museum, what will happen to the copies?"

"No doubt they will be disputed over for some time to come, especially as the Museum didn't sanction them in the first place."

"Still, Sayidi, at least we were paid for our efforts this time."

I nod, though I know that money is no salve against the pain of personal loss.

13

The Sahara Bugle Gazette Tuesday 8th April 1969

Defendant Shot and Killed During Prominent Murder Trial

In a violent turn of events yesterday during the trial of disgraced head of the Museum of Antiquities, Doctor Marious J. Keyatta (the defendant), was shot and killed while giving evidence. The woman, Ms Anita Purkell, half-sister of the murdered Dante Purkell, waited until Doctor Keyatta had finished giving his account of the affair, before using a small automatic pistol to fire three shots. The first two hit Doctor Keyatta in the chest, while the second caught him in the head, from which he died instantly. Ms Purkell then proceeded to surrender herself to court officials, and was led from the court by two armed gendarmes.

The Usual Unusual Suspects

Alice Rothwell was one of the original MIPsters. She has taught Special Needs pupils for decades, and is now retired to a life of babysitting grandchildren, crochet and the occasional piece for various community magazines. Her first question when we contacted her was: "How the hell did you get hold of my phone number?!"

Dave Perry was another original MIPster, though between work and his wonderfully energetic family, he has written "bugger all" for quite some time. ***Breakdown on the Galactic Highway*** originally won the Hilltop Press award, and is reprinted here from the pages of Boopledoggin' Magazine – part of The Electronic Apa (see *The Beast of EAYOR* available free at www.smashwords.com/books/view/1015984)

Kelly Lewis comes from Devon, likes long walks and cats, detests telephone cold callers, dogs, and certain people who use the expression 'Janner' within her hearing. Her work has appeared in various magazines, including **The Hub, Bottle, 3 x 5** and **Expressions** to name a few.

Dan Meyers sadly passed away in 2018 after becoming the victim of a massive stroke, from which he never recovered. We first made contact in a writer's forum in 2015, where he asked questions, then asked if I would become his beta reader. The pieces were not quick in coming – he owned and worked a farm in the US, but wrote during the winter periods when he had a fraction more spare time to do so. The two pieces here were originally destined for a proper anthology of his work, to be titled **Tales from the Travelling Carnival**. We hope to reprint them individually in the Crimeucopia series.

John Connor has been writing and publishing under a menagerie of names since the late 1970s – sometimes even professionally. He has worked at a variety of jobs, in a variety of locations, and has published amateur, small press, and semi-pro magazines in the past. Sadly, without medication, he's at it again.

W. G. Johnson wishes to remain off the grid.

Please note – The 1st Edition of **California Twist** is in the process of being repackaged. The 1st Edition will be retired shortly, once the 2nd Edition (with a new cover by **Dana Thompson** of **DTKinetic**) has been set up with IngramSpark.

Turncoat and **Detritus** will remain unchanged for the present.